THE ODDS
ON
MURDER

GW00470747

THE ODDS ON MURDER

an Inspector Constable murder mystery

by

Roger Keevil

To Patsy, the finest horse in the business, from Arthur

Printed by CreateSpace, An Amazon.com
Company
Available on Kindle and other devices

Chapter 1

To a resounding flourish from the State Trumpeters, the carriage procession turned into the Royal Enclosure in front of the main stand at Goodwell Park. The opening day of the Glamorous Goodwell race meeting was under way.

*

"Copper, isn't it?"

Detective Sergeant Dave Copper, a fraction over medium height and, to his regret, a fraction more over medium weight, looked up from his race card to find himself being addressed by a slightly stooped but still tall individual, immaculate in formal dress. The silver hair was crowned with a gleaming silk top hat. The craggy face, with a hawk-like nose and a pair of piercing grey eyes, wore the tan of an outdoors-man. "Er ... that's right."

"Thought so. Try never to forget a face, you know. Specially when they've done me a good turn, so to speak."

"It's ... er ... it's very good of you to say so." Copper tried not to let it show on his face that he was desperately racking his brains to identify the other man.

"And I don't know if you're aware, but we got all the pictures back in the end. Every single one of them. Even the Tintoretto. Undamaged. Thanks to some smart work by you and your colleagues."

The penny dropped. "We managed to round up the whole gang, sir. And it wasn't just your house they targeted. It was a pretty big operation. I was just a small cog in the machine."

"Well, anyway, caught sight of you, and just thought I'd mention my appreciation." The older man looked over his shoulder to where a mature woman, elegantly clad in cream lace and wearing one of her signature feather-trimmed cartwheel hats, could be heard discoursing knowledgeably in her deep voice as to the merits of a passing thoroughbred to a much younger man and a small group of fluttering attendants. "And now I'd better get back to HRH before she completely intimidates my grandson." He held out a grey-gloved hand. "Good to have seen you again, Mr. Copper." A glance at the two men standing alongside the sergeant. "I hope you and your friends enjoy yourselves."

Copper took the proffered hand. "Thank you, my lord."

"Who on earth was that old boy?" enquired one of Copper's companions, regarding the retreating back in some astonishment.

"Bit more respect from you, young Pete, if you don't mind," replied Copper, grinning at the expression on his friend's face. "You're standing on that old boy's grass. That just happens to be the Earl of Warke. He owns the racecourse."

"So how come you know an earl, for crying out loud?" was the incredulous reaction of the third of the trio. "Bit above your pay grade, isn't it?"

Copper smiled. "It's all perfectly simple, Matt. You probably don't remember that case a while back when a gang was going around stealing pictures from country houses? It could have been before you joined up. It was before I got made up to sergeant, and I was still in Intelligence. Anyway, I got sent to

Lord Warke's place after he had the break-in, and I happened to be the one who took his statement. That's all."

"So we don't have to bow and scrape and call you 'sir'?" laughed his colleague.

"Not just yet," responded Copper. "Mind you, watch out when I pass my inspector's exams!" An announcement over the loudspeaker system interrupted proceedings to draw the crowd's attention to the start of the next race, and the three joined the general drift towards the rails. "Anyway, enough shop. Let's see if we can win some money."

*

"It's a mug's game, you know."

"Guv?" Dave Copper looked up from his keyboard, glad of the opportunity to take a break from entering a mind-numbing series of statistics into a crime report which, he suspected, probably nobody would ever read.

"What you were going on about earlier," said Detective Inspector Andy Constable. He took a sip from the mug of tea in front of him and pushed away the pile of files on his desk, leaned his long frame back in his chair, stretched out his legs, and raised his arms expansively, only to stop short with a sudden 'Ow!'.

"You okay, guv?"

"Yes, I'm fine," grunted Constable. "I just forget sometimes, that's all, and it catches me. Don't worry about it."

"And it's ages since you had the stitches out, isn't it?"

"And that will teach me not to get in the way

of a knife-wielding maniac, won't it, sergeant?" said Constable with a smile at his junior. "As I said at the time, I shall be leaving all the dangerous stuff to you in future. Anyway, as I recall, we weren't talking about me. We were talking about you and your determination to dive headlong into penury as the result of an uncontrollable gambling habit."

"I'm not sure I'd put it quite like that, sir," protested Copper. "It's only a bit of fun."

"You say that now," replied Constable. "That's how it starts. Just you bear in mind that chap at the Queen's Theatre and the trouble he got into."

"I'd hardly call a couple of quid in the station sweepstake on the winner of the Five Thousand Guineas an uncontrollable gambling habit, guv. Anyway, I seem to remember you buying a ticket in the sweep for the Grand National."

"Yes," agreed Constable, "and where did it get me? Nowhere. Blasted animal chucked off its jockey at the second fence, and then carried on blithely round the entire course, getting in everyone else's way, and then crossing the line first, looking maddeningly pleased with itself."

"Yes, but if the jockey had managed to stay on board, you'd have scooped the pool, sir."

"Too many ifs, Copper. I should have learnt the lessons of my youth."

"How do you mean, guv?"

The inspector flexed his shoulder as if to ease out the last of the discomfort. "I remember when I was a little kid. We quite often used to go round to my grandparents' on a Saturday morning. Well, there was always cake. My grandmother was the most brilliant cook. A couple of my uncles used to play for the village football team, and quite often in the winter the whole family would go and watch them on a Saturday afternoon, and then we'd go back and my grandmother would put on a huge sit-down tea for about fifteen or twenty of us." A sigh of reminiscence.

"Don't quite see where this fits in with the gambling, sir."

"Ah. No. I digress. Back to Saturday mornings. Because whenever we got there, there would be my grandad, together with a couple of uncles ..."

"Same uncles?"

"Big family," smiled Constable. "Plus a couple of family friends who were sort of courtesy uncles. Anyway, there they would all be, gathered around the dining table in a cloud of cigarette smoke, morning papers spread out all over the cloth, open at the racing pages, and they'd be poring over all the details, talking about form and picking out their fancies. Very intense stuff – I swear Eisenhower and his generals had less trouble planning D-Day. And then once the decisions had been made, off someone would go to the betting shop, list of runners and bundle of banknotes in hand, to place the bets. And then they'd all be glued to the television all afternoon."

"And the result was ...?"

"The result was very much what you'd expect it to be. The bundle of banknotes which came back from the bookies' at the end of the day was almost always considerably smaller than the bundle which went. But there was at least one positive outcome."

"What was that, then, sir?"

"Grandad and the uncles got to be quite close friends with the bookie. He used to turn up in his Jag every so often with a bottle of scotch. I think he must have been grateful to the family for helping to keep him in the style to which he had become accustomed. So be warned, young David!" intoned Constable in solemn accents, a smile taking the seriousness out of his words. "There tends to be only one winner in the horse-racing world, and it probably isn't you."

"I shall take the warning to heart, sir," grinned Copper. "Although I still reckon a day at the races isn't going to wreck me financially."

"And you're going with ...?"

"Couple of guys from the control room, guv. Pete Radley and Matt Cawston."

"Those reprobates," muttered Constable. "Well then, you deserve all you get."

Copper elected not to hear the comment. "Anyway, we got chatting in the canteen, after they'd sold me the ticket. They said they were going on the day, and why didn't I come along? And I had a day off due, and I've never actually been to the races before, so I thought, why not?"

"So you'll be there, sat on your tartan blanket, eating ham sandwiches and guzzling cans of lager."

"Hardly, guv. Nothing but the best. Pete knows someone who knows someone, and he's managed to wangle us some tickets for the VIP enclosure. Formal gear, the lot."

Andy Constable, who had been taking a further sip of his tea, very nearly choked. "You in a

10

top hat?" he spluttered in incredulity. "Now that is a sight I would pay good money to see!"

"Then you'd better check out Facebook on the day, hadn't you, sir?" responded Copper a touch huffily, unconsciously ruffling his already tousled hair even further. "I expect the guys will be posting some photos."

"Looks as if this couple of quid of yours is going to turn into quite an expensive outing, if you're going to be hiring formal togs," remarked Constable. "I'm assuming you don't have a topper stashed away at the top of the wardrobe alongside your old uniform helmet?"

"As it happens, guv, Pete got us a very good group hire rate from the shop in the precinct. And the tickets get us free entry to the hospitality marquee, so we're good to go."

"Well, in that case, I can't see that I can possibly have any objections," chuckled Constable. "When is it again?"

"Next Wednesday, guv."

"Well, we'll struggle through without you somehow. But in the meantime, shouldn't you be getting back to that fascinating pile of figures in front of you?"

"What, as my penance in advance for daring to go off and enjoy myself, sir? Is that it?"

"Something of the sort, sergeant. But I dare say you'll get your reward in heaven."

"Lucky old me, sir." Copper bent his head once more to his task. "I'd settle for just one winner at decent odds."

*

"Can't help it, guys," beamed a delighted Dave Copper as he turned back to his friends, a small but satisfying wad of banknotes in his hand. "Put it down to beginner's luck."

"That's twice you've done that," grunted Pete Radley, crumpling his worthless betting slip as the three walked away from the bank of on-course bookmakers.

"Yes, but only because I won by accident on the first one," countered Copper. "I said I was just going to have one bet for fun and then pack it in. And then I only picked the first one because I liked the name."

"'Run Rabbit Run'!" scoffed Matt Cawston. "Daft name for a horse! And no form at all. And then the blasted thing comes in at 20-1! And by rights, with that pedigree, it should still be running at half past five."

"Ah, the old jokes are the best," retorted Copper, in no way put down by his colleagues' reactions to his good fortune. "Anyway, guys, I did give the bookie a chance to get some of his money back. It's not my fault if 'Smack The Pony' did the business as well. And it was only 5-1 this time, so I reckon this is as good a time to pack it in as any, before my luck runs out completely. I'm not a believer in the old 'never-two-without-three' theory. And in any case, I've already got a horse in the Five Thousand Guineas, haven't I?"

"What was it you drew again?" asked Pete.

"Something called 'Last Edition'. Don't know a thing about it. I meant to look it up on the net when I drew the name at the station, but I forgot."

"Who's up?"

"Up?"

Pete cast his eyes upwards and tutted. "Remind me never to take you racing again. I mean who's the jockey?"

"Oh. I do remember that. Chap called Elliott. But I didn't look him up either. Sorry."

"Hmmm. He's not bad," said Pete. "Middling sort of form. I don't think he's ever won anything special. Bit like the horse, really. Unlike mine. Brilliant animal. So don't get your hopes up, because 'Teddy The Bear' is going to walk it."

"And I've got 'Stumblebum'," reported Matt glumly, "so I might as well go home now. That thing couldn't win a race if you fed it rocket fuel."

Copper laughed. "So we've got one 'yes', one 'no', and one 'don't know'. That sounds like a reasonable spread of possibilities." He glanced at his watch. "You know, all this winning gives a man a thirst. If you're not fussed about watching the next one, what say we repair to the hospitality marquee, and I'll treat us to a little snifter before the big race?"

"Repair? A snifter?" echoed Pete incredulously. "What sort of language is that? You sound like something out of a Bertie Wooster story. I reckon you've been working with your guv'nor for too long. Either that, or you're mixing with too many earls."

"So you don't fancy a jar?"

"Did I say that?" grinned Pete in reply. "And as it's your treat. Come on, Constable Cawston. It's not very often you get a sergeant offering to stand you a drink. You might as well take advantage of it."

He led the way in the direction of the large white marquee whose proudly-fluttering red-and-gold banners announced the fact that 'De Sade Champagne is honoured to sponsor the 5000 Guineas Steeplechase'.

Inside the tent, a profusion of crystal chandeliers, enormous and opulent flower arrangements, swathes of pink and white fabric draped across to form a ceiling, and a generous scatter of tables and chairs adorned with brocade cloths and bows, created the impression that there was about to be a society wedding reception on the lawns of a great country house. A hubbub arose from the large throng filling the marquee, the women in dresses ranging from the chic to the bizarre, with hats to match which ran the gamut from the tiniest and most frivolous feathered fascinators to huge constructions of straw and chiffon which looked as if they required neck muscles of iron to support. By contrast, the ladies' escorts were almost uniformly drab in their grey and black formal wear, with only here and there a vivid waistcoat or coloured stock to enliven the picture. Waiters clad in the red-and-gold colours of the sponsoring house circulated in a perpetual ballet, bearing trays laden with glasses of champagne.

"Good afternoon, gentlemen," smiled the tall and impossibly glamorous blonde hostess at the entrance, after a discreet glance to ensure that the visitors' badges entitled them to admission to her privileged domain. "Welcome to the De Sade Marquee. Please make yourselves comfortable. If you would like some refreshments, please take a seat and one of my colleagues will be happy to serve you from the buffet. And of course the complimentary bar is at your disposal, if by chance you prefer something other than champagne."

"I'm guessing," murmured Copper to his colleagues, as they made their way towards the bar which stretched the full length of one side of the marquee, "that your usual half of bitter may not be on offer here."

"And once again you fall on your feet," observed Pete. "This generous offer to buy us drinks out of your winnings is going to cost you absolutely zilch. And since young Matt here so very kindly volunteered to do the driving today ..."

"Oh, lucky me," murmured the junior officer.

"... I shall treat myself to something very large and expensive. Let's see what they've got."

"What may I get for you, sirs?" The enquiry came in a slight French accent from the young barman who stood polishing a glass behind the bar.

Copper surveyed the immense array of bottles displayed on the bar shelves. "Er ... I have no idea. Pete, how about you?"

"Give me a sec," replied his colleague. "I'm still looking. I haven't seen this much alcohol since I went backup on a raid with Customs on a booze smuggler's warehouse."

"Matt?"

"I suppose I'd better just have an orange juice," came the dispirited reply.

The barman smiled in sympathy. "Ah. You will be the designated driver then, sir?"

"We gave the chauffeur the day off," remarked Pete, his eyes still ranging along the selection of drinks on offer.

"I think we can do better than just an orange juice, sir," said the barman. "Perhaps, if it will be just the one, I could suggest a Buck's Fizz. You cannot be expected to miss out on the champagne completely, as it is all on the house."

"Sounds good to me," said Matt, mollified.

"And for you, sir?" asked the barman, as he passed the glass across the bar. "If not a champagne, perhaps you would like something a little stronger. We have some very fine whiskies and cognacs, or perhaps a cocktail ...?"

"Ummm ..." Copper continued to look perplexed.

The barman took pity on him. "If I may suggest, sir, would you like to try our cocktail of the day? It has been specially created by our master sommelier M. Philippe Gilbert for today's meeting, and it is named in honour of the famous racehorse Nijinsky. And it has been very popular, and not just with the ladies, but with the gentlemen too. Would you like to try that?"

"Maybe." Copper didn't sound too sure. "What's in it?"

"It is of course based on our classic Domaine De Sade Brut champagne, sir," explained the barman, "and to that we add a measure of cognac, some triple sec, a little white rum ..."

"Shame it's not Red Rum!" quipped Pete.

"... and a dash of Angostura bitters."

"Sounds all right," said Copper. "Okay, I'll give

it a try. A Nijinsky it is. And make it two. If I'm going to be standing here drinking a poncey cocktail, Pete, I'm not doing it alone."

"You'd better make it three," laughed Pete. "Then Matt here can give his to his horse, and it might actually make it over the first fence!"

The cocktail proved surprisingly enjoyable. So much so that it was followed by another, and a pattern might easily have developed, had not the public address system announced that preparations for the signature race of the day, the Five Thousand Guineas, were under way, with the runners already parading in the paddock. Many of those in the marquee gravitated, champagne glasses in hand, towards the large television screens set up at each end of the tent, but the majority of the crowd, the three police officers among them, made their way outside, determined to experience the full atmosphere and excitement of the event.

"So where's the best place to watch from?" enquired Dave Copper.

"Well, you can forget the stands," replied Pete. "No chance of getting up there on a day like today. I quite fancy trying to get somewhere on the rails. You can still watch the race on the big screens, but you get a terrific rush when the horses actually go past you."

"You're the expert," acknowledged Copper. "You'd better lead on."

To their surprise, the trio managed to carve out a space in the crush virtually next to the winning post. As the hour of the race approached, the excitement grew. Bells rang. The cries from the bookmakers' stalls grew ever-louder and more insistent. A thudding of hooves signalled the passing of the participants as they cantered up from the paddock to the start. The public address system rang out with constant updates as to the state of readiness of the runners. For a brief moment, there was an almost preternatural silence. And then, with a sudden all-enveloping roar, the crowd gave voice as the field burst out of the starting gates.

Copper, torn between watching the race on the screen on the other side of the track and craning his neck for a glimpse of the action, found himself swept up in the excitement as the runners flashed past on their first circuit of the course and he managed to catch sight of the purple-and-orange colours of Last Edition's jockey. The pitch of the commentator's voice over the loudspeakers grew steadily higher. Every so often, the crowd seemed to hold its collective breath as the horses crashed through another hurdle. A groan arose as one of the more fancied runners failed to find its feet at one of the fences and tumbled in a welter of horseflesh and humanity, while its competitors passed on relentlessly. As the horses approached the finish, four of them virtually in line abreast, the cacophony grew as they thundered past, to be replaced by a loud hum of speculation as it became clear that there was no obvious winner. Seconds later, the announcement came that the result would be decided by a photograph. As the hum grew ever louder, and the three police officers exchanged shrugs, the loudspeakers crackled into life again.

"The result of the De Sade Five Thousand

Guineas Steeplechase is as follows. First, by a short head, 'Last Edition', owned by Mrs. J. Baverstock, trained by Sir Richard Effingham, and ridden by Owen Elliott. Second, ..."

The rest of the announcement was lost in a huge burst of cheering. Dave Copper jumped in the air with a whoop of triumph, before flinging his arms around each of his colleagues in turn in bear-hugs of joy. "Bloody marvellous! Three out of three! Hey, guys, this is fun. You'd better let me know next time you're coming to the races – I might want to tag along."

"Not likely, mate," snorted Pete with a grudging laugh. "You're too good at this. You soak up all the luck. I'll tell you what, though – you can pick out horses for us for the rest of the afternoon, as long as you promise not to have a bet yourself."

"Deal!" grinned Copper, his face still wreathed in an exuberant smile. "So what do you reckon we go back to the marquee, and I'll see if I can sort you out some winners over another drink? And I'll tell you what, Matt – it's not so very far to get home, and a taxi's not going to cost an arm and a leg. Why don't you and Pete whistle up a mate or two from uniform, and get them to pop over and take your car home for you? Highly irregular, but I won't tell the Chief Constable if you don't, and then I'll stand us a cab out of my winnings, and you can have a drink to help me celebrate."

"Now that," smiled his colleague, "is what I call a result."

Chapter 2

"He's done what?" A laugh of disbelief. "No, you're right, ma'am ... no, it's not funny at all. So when do you want me to ...?" Andy Constable's eyebrows rose in surprise. "Straight away? No, of course that's not a problem. There's nothing on my desk that won't keep. I can easily put things aside." He glanced down at the pile of paperwork in front of him and suppressed a sigh of relief. "So will I be working on my own with D.I. Warner's team? ... Well, that would be very helpful, ma'am, if I can take him with me ... Yes, I quite understand the sensitivity. I'll get on to it straight away."

Constable replaced the receiver and turned to Dave Copper with a smile on his face. "You know how much you've been enjoying doing those analyses I delegated to you?"

"The ones you said formed an essential part of my career progression, sir?" replied Copper wryly. "Yes, guv. I'm having a really good time sorting them out."

"Dump 'em," said Constable shortly. "We have other fish to fry. Or to be more exact, horses."

"You what, guv?"

Constable rose, shrugged his way into his jacket, and reached for his car keys. "Tell you on the way to the car. We're off to Effingham Hall at Knaggs End."

Copper stood. "Isn't that a bit off our patch, guv?" he enquired, as he followed his superior along the corridor. "That's the far side of Westchester, over the other side of the county."

"Indeed it is, sergeant. Well spotted. But by a stroke of luck, we have a chance for an awayday in the beautiful English countryside, doing what they actually pay us to do. I say luck – not so much luck for D.I. Warner, whose case this was supposed to be. He's just got himself carted off to hospital, courtesy of a broken femur."

"How come?"

"Kicked by a horse." The officers exchanged glances before bursting out into laughter.

"You what?"

"On the scene of the crime, for some reason. Further details still to be obtained. But it's not what you expect in an average policeman's working day, so I couldn't stop myself having a chuckle. Although, as the Chief Superintendent pointed out, murder is no laughing matter." The two reached Constable's car and climbed in.

"So what's it all about then, guv?" asked Copper, as the inspector pulled into the traffic and set a course for the bypass.

"We have a titled corpse on our hands. One of the great and the good, it seems. Hence the sensitivity which the Chief Super was so eager to stress. One Sir Richard Effingham."

Copper's attention was alerted. "Hang on, guv. That name seems to ring something of a bell. Just let me ..." He reached into his pocket, produced his phone, and started dabbing at the screen. "Got it! He's a racehorse trainer. I knew I knew the name. In fact, he was the guy who trained 'Last Edition' – the horse I won the station sweepstake on."

"That's good, then," replied his superior.

"You'll have the inside track on everything, won't you?"

"Ouch! Does that mean we're going to get horse jokes all day, sir?"

"I sincerely hope not, sergeant. But that's rather more your forte than mine, so I hope you'll manage to rein yourself in."

"Just sitting here quietly, guv," said Copper, face admirably straight. As he continued to peruse the screen, his attention was caught by a further item. "Hang on a minute, sir ... there's something else here." He read on, and his expression changed to one of sadness. "Well, there's a thing."

"And what's that?"

"That horse, sir. 'Last Edition'."

"Your lucky winner?"

"Not so lucky after all, as it turned out, guv. It's dead."

"Dead? That's a bit sudden, isn't it? If it was jumping about and winning races not so long ago. What did it die of?"

Copper read on. "Doesn't say exactly, sir. Something about an accident during training. It's all a bit vague. Shame, though. I bet that horse was worth a fortune after that win."

"Well, I hope to goodness they're not going to have us investigating the death of the horse as well as the trainer," remarked Constable drily. "One suspicious death at a time is quite enough for me." He turned off the main road and began to navigate the twisting cross-country lanes in the direction of Knaggs End.

As the car breasted the final rise before

descending into the tree-filled valley which marked their destination, a huge vista opened before them. Vast stretches of chalk downs spread to the horizon, punctuated with hedgerows dividing fields clad in the gold and green of cereals and arable crops, with occasional prehistoric burial mounds rising like islands in a rippling sea of foliage. Here and there, a great oak provided a solitary punctuation mark. On the skyline, the distinctive furrowed silhouette of an ancient hill fort stood sentinel. And over all, the gigantic bowl of a pale blue sky, dotted with a scattering of white clouds in a stately but relentless march towards the eastern horizon, presided calmly over a perfect English summer's day. Below in the valley, the spire of Knaggs End church rose through the canopy of greenery, and as the road descended, the trees began to close in, until the officers reached an imposing stone-flanked gateway, its pillars crowned with horse-head sculptures, with a small stone-built lodge of a vaguely Jacobean design standing to one side. The drive, shadowed by massive specimen trees and lined with a profusion of rhododendrons in exuberant bloom, suddenly emerged into the broad gravel sweep which fronted the south face of Effingham Hall.

"Bloody hell!" ejaculated Copper. "It's Castle Dracula!"

Effingham Hall was a perfect example of Victorian gothic architecture at the height of its flowering. Mullioned oriel windows gazed up aslant at crenellated parapets, where heraldic beasts sat, proudly supporting shields bearing the stony coat-of-arms of the Effingham family. Courses of brick and stone climbed upwards towards fairy-tale slate-crowned turrets. Climbing plants, their leaves a rich and glossy red, scrambled up and over an imposing *porte-cochère*, large enough to take the grandest of carriages, in an attempt to soften its formidable outlines. The Hall stood on a low platform, with glimpses of urn-flanked paved terraces visible to right and left. And before the house, somewhat detracting from its calm and stately image, stood a scatter of police vehicles.

The detectives climbed the steps to the door of the house, where a uniformed officer stood. "D.I. Constable and D.S. Copper," said the inspector, as the pair flashed their warrant cards. "I believe we're looking for Sergeant Fletcher."

"Oh, yes, sir," replied the P.C. "We were warned to expect you. He's just inside – I think you'll find him in the billiard room. Just through there, sir, second on the left."

"Billiard room, eh?" murmured Copper, as the two followed the directions. "How the rich do live."

Entering the billiard room, the detectives were met with the sight of the back of a man, bent over the billiard table as he examined a selection of items spread out on a sheet on its surface. "D.S. Fletcher, I presume," said Constable.

The other turned in surprise. "Inspector, sir. Am I glad to see you! The Super sent a message to say that they were sending you over to take charge. And thank goodness, because we've just been on hold since they had to take D.I. Warner away."

"What exactly happened?" asked Constable. "All I know is that it's got something to do with a horse."

"It's partly my fault, sir," admitted Fletcher. "We got here first thing, to carry on after making a start last night, and while we were waiting for the doctor to arrive to take a look at the victim, I asked Inspector Warner if it would be a good idea if we used the time to take a look around the place, just to get an idea of the general set-up. It's my first murder case, you see," he continued, "so I hoped I might be able to learn a few things from the inspector's thoughts."

"Hear that, Copper?" remarked Constable. "A sergeant who wants to learn a few tips from his inspector. Now there's a novel idea." Copper just grinned in response.

"Anyway, sir," went on the slightly nonplussed Fletcher, "we went out to the back of the house – what they call the stable yard. Well, there is actually a stable there, and that's where they keep the horse."

"Just the one? I thought the dead man was a racehorse trainer."

"Oh, apparently the racehorses are kept somewhere else, sir. No, this one's owned by the lady of the house. I understand she goes riding. And Mr. Warner, he fancies himself as someone who knows a bit about horses, so he went into the stable to make friends with the horse."

"And I'm guessing the horse had other ideas?"

"Yes, sir. The D.I. went round the back of it, and the thing let out with a great big kick, and before I knew where I was, there's Mr. Warner lying on the ground yelling blue murder, and some old bloke who I think is some sort of gardener came running and got the horse out of the way. And then the doctor turned up, and he took a look and said the inspector's leg was broken, so he stayed with him until the ambulance came and took him away. And in between groans, Mr. Warner said we'd better get someone in to take over, so I called in. And here you are, thank goodness."

"Well, nice to be appreciated," said Constable. "So, why don't you bring us up to speed with everything else. What do we know so far?"

Fletcher drew a notebook from his pocket and consulted it. "The dead man is Sir Richard Effingham, sir. Fifth baronet, apparently, whatever that might be. We got a call last night at 8.29pm, and there happened to be a car not too far away, so they attended about ten minutes later. They found the body in the library ..."

Constable sighed. "I suppose we may as well get all the clichés out of the way as early as possible. I suppose the next thing you'll be telling me is that there's a butler."

"Er-hrrm." The discreet cough came from the doorway. "Excuse me, sir, but her ladyship has asked me to enquire whether the police ..." There was the faintest of hesitations. "... gentlemen would like some refreshments."

"And you are ...?"

"Pelham, sir," replied the tail-coated newcomer. "Her ladyship's butler. She wondered if you would you care for some coffee? Or perhaps some mugs of tea."

"Um ... not just at the moment, thank you," replied Constable abstractedly. "We are rather busy. Perhaps later."

"Very good, sir. I shall be serving coffee to her ladyship at eleven o'clock, in the morning room. Perhaps that would be a more convenient time for you." Pelham faded back into the gloom of the entrance hall.

"Is that bloke genuine?" gurgled Copper. "He's like something out of an old film. He must be about a hundred years old. And get those side-whiskers!"

"Never mind about the whiskers," retorted Constable. "At the moment, I'm more concerned about our murder victim. Obviously he is a murder victim, Fletcher? Otherwise we wouldn't all be standing around his billiard table."

"Very much so, sir. The body was discovered after everyone heard a shot, and there are injuries to the body which pretty much rule out any other interpretation. Even I could see that, sir. Inspector Warner and I came in last night to take a look at the scene, but for some reason, we couldn't get the doctor here straight away, so everything was just sealed off with a couple of officers standing guard until this morning. And you know what happened then."

"And so what did the doctor say?"

"Dr. Livermore, sir? You can ask him yourself, sir. He's still next door with the body."

"In which case, what on earth are we still doing here?" enquired Constable in reasonable tones which contained only the faintest edge of irritation. "Come on, Fletcher. You know the layout. Lead on."

As the three officers entered the library, a stout man, tweed-suited with rubicund features and a bristling moustache, was just straightening up from an examination of the body, which remained seated, oddly upright, its back to them, in the high-backed chair behind a large mahogany partners' desk standing in the centre of the room, the chair facing away from the desk towards the window.

"Ah. At last. You have the air of a senior investigating officer. Just what I need."

"And you will be Dr. Livermore, I presume," smiled the inspector. He held out a hand. "D.I. Constable ... this is my sergeant, D.S. Copper ... drafted in after Mr. Warner's unfortunate accident."

"Yes," grunted the doctor. "Damn fool. Should have known better than to go sneaking around the back of a horse. Townies, you see. Know nothing. Only got what was coming to him."

"Oh. Right," said Constable, sounding somewhat disconcerted by the other's unfeeling reaction. "But I'm hoping the same thing isn't the case with our unfortunate victim here."

"Couldn't tell you, inspector. In fact, there are too many things that I can't tell you for my liking."

"Meaning what exactly, doctor?"

"Well, don't just stand there, man. Come and take a look at the fellow, and you'll see what I mean."

"Shouldn't we be kitting up, doctor?" asked Constable. "Overalls, and so on. The last thing we'd want to do would be to contaminate the crime scene and compromise your investigations."

Dr. Livermore waved his hand dismissively. "Load of rubbish! I don't bother with nonsense like that. If I can't tell the difference between traces that are relevant and the paw-marks left by some grubby-handed plod after all the years I've been doing this job, they ought to put me out to grass here and now. So, don't hover there in the background. Come and see the situation for yourself. But I have to tell you that I don't like it. I don't like it one little bit."

Constable, the other officers in tow, rounded the desk to view the murdered man. He saw an individual apparently in his mid-sixties, with a mane of dark grey hair, his face frozen in a startled expression with staring open blue eyes. The body was formally clad in a dinner jacket, with a black bow tie and a crisply-pleated dress shirt, whose pristine whiteness was disfigured by a bloodstain surrounding the blade of an oriental dagger, its hilt dully gleaming with jewels, which had been driven into the corpse's chest.

"Not too much doubt about the cause of death, then, guv," remarked Copper in an aside to his superior.

"Don't you be too sure of that, sergeant," barked the doctor. "They ought to teach you young officers not to jump to conclusions before you know all the facts."

"Youthful exuberance, I'm afraid, doctor," said Constable. "I'm forever telling him not to rush his fences. So please, enlighten us, what are all the facts?"

"Can't tell you yet," replied the doctor. "And don't expect me to be drawn until I've had a chance to have a good look at him on the slab. Which I might have been well on the way towards, if I hadn't had to hang about waiting for you to arrive so that I could show you everything *in situ*, so to speak. So, look here. If you'd been paying attention, sergeant, you might have noticed that the dagger wound isn't the only thing amiss with this chap. See all these holes here in the jacket and shirt – that's from the spray of pellets from a shotgun blast, or I'm a Dutchman."

"Shotgun?" echoed Copper, bewildered. "Isn't that a bit of overkill, guv? I mean, if he's been shot, why stab him? And if he's been stabbed, why shoot him?"

"My point exactly, young man," nodded the doctor. "Now you begin to see why I'm not happy."

"I did say there was a shot heard, sir," interposed Fletcher. "That was what alerted the household and led to our being called in."

"Thank you, Fletcher. And do we have the weapon?"

"Not a sign of it so far, sir. They're searching."

"Good." Constable turned back to the doctor. "So, two wounds, then."

"And again, jumping to conclusions, inspector," countered the doctor. "You're as bad as your sergeant. Come round here and take a look at this."

Constable moved to the other side of the body as the doctor indicated. "Ouch."

"Not strictly medical terminology," said Dr.

30

Livermore, "but in essence, you're correct. That blow to the head could well have caused serious cranial trauma. The classic blunt instrument, by the look of things. Can't tell you any more than that at the moment, but once I've opened him up I'll be able to be rather more forthcoming."

"But could that have been fatal, doctor?" enquired Copper.

"Hold your horses, sergeant. You'll know when I know."

"So is that everything, then, doc?" ventured Constable warily.

"Not quite. See the throat?" The doctor indicated marks visible above the shirt collar.

"Strangulation?" The disbelief was plain to hear in the inspector's voice. "Oh, come on!"

"I only know what I see," responded the doctor. "Bruising, discolouration, call it what you will, but it ought not to be there. And those marks aren't caused by the human hand. Wrong spacing and so on, and I don't see the variations in pressure that I'd expect. Probably some kind of ligature, but don't quote me yet until I've taken a closer look. But you might like to have your forensics people take a look around for something about three-quarters of an inch wide, with some sort of figured or textured surface."

"SOCO are on the hunt, sir," intervened Fletcher once again. "They've come up with a couple of things so far, but they're still working."

"Right. We'll get to them in due course. So, doctor, is there anything else?"

"Isn't that enough?" retorted the doctor. "So,

now you've seen everything I've seen, and with your kind permission, I'm going to have this chap taken away so that I can get on with my proper work, and leave the speculation to you people."

"By all means, doctor," said Constable.

"Good. Then I'll have my staff bag him up and get him into their van. It'll give them something productive to do, instead of hanging about waiting for the C.I.D."

"Apologies for the delay, doctor," said the inspector smoothly. "But I gather that my colleagues from this area weren't able to get in touch with you last night."

"I should think not. Considering the price of opera tickets these days, I was damned if I was going to have my enjoyment of *Tosca* ruined by a little thing like work, so I made sure my phone was firmly switched off. And it stayed that way until this morning." Dr. Livermore bent to pick up his bag. "If that's all, inspector, I'll be on my way."

"Any idea when I might expect your report, doctor?" enquired Constable.

"As soon as I've finished writing it," replied the doctor shortly. "Check your emails." With a curt nod, he was gone.

"Now there's a cheery chappie," commented Copper in an undertone. "Not quite the jolly approach we're used to from our own doc, was it, guv?"

"You're right there, sergeant," agreed Constable. "Evidently a horse of a very different colour from the doc back at base. Makes you realise when you're well off. Still, as long as he's good at his job." He sighed. "Which brings us back to this poor chap here." He stood looking at the dead man in silence for several moments. "Sir Richard Effingham," he mused, half to himself. He glanced around the room. "Evidently well off. Racehorse trainer, you say, Copper, so that would reinforce the impression that he moved in moneyed circles." He moved across to the french windows and gazed out at the terrace and the formal gardens below. "I wonder, do we have to start looking there for motives?"

"I'm guessing that we might be able to rule out robbery, sir," suggested Copper. "Take a look at this lot." He indicated a large glass-topped cabinet standing to one side of the library in front of a range of bookshelves.

Constable examined the cabinet. Inside, cushioned on velvet, lay a selection of exquisite objects, all seemingly of oriental origin. Pale ivory figures with serene expressions and flowing robes kept company with delicate pieces of multi-coloured *cloisonné*. A miniature menagerie of carved jade animals in a rainbow of shades was flanked by intricately-worked representations of Indian deities in sandalwood and rose quartz. Mesopotamian cylinder seals lay alongside beautifully-crafted Japanese netsukes portraying caricatures of labouring peasants and mythical creatures. In pride of place lay a gold hair adornment featuring quivering bees hovering above tiny flowers on infinitesimal springs. "That," remarked the inspector, "is a very impressive collection."

"And you can't help noticing," pointed out

Copper, "that there's something of a gap in the centre, just under that gold comb thing. Something that's maybe more or less the size and shape of that dagger in the dead man's chest?"

"You are absolutely right, sergeant," agreed Constable. "Well spotted. So, we'll definitely need SOCO to take a look at that. Fletcher, here's a job for you. Go and track down someone from the SOCO team, and get them to have that dagger removed from the body for detailed examination. Under the doctor's supervision, of course! We don't want to get on the wrong side of him any more than we have to. Off you go, quick as you can."

"Will do, sir." Fletcher hurried from the room.

"What I still don't get, guv," said Copper, " is why whoever did this didn't just stab Sir Richard with the dagger and leave it at that. Okay, the doc's not giving anything away, but it looks to me as if that knife was quite enough to finish the guy off. To do all this, our murderer must have really hated him with a vengeance. I mean, they really wanted him dead, didn't they?"

Constable smiled grimly. "There certainly seems no doubt about that, sergeant. But I tend to agree with Dr. Livermore. There's something odd about it all, and I also don't like it one little bit."

"So we fall back on the old routine, do we, sir? The trusty search for means, motive, and opportunity? Even though the means seem pretty obvious."

"I think we may have to go further than that. I think we'll be taking a leaf out of Kipling's book."

Copper looked puzzled. "I don't understand,

sir. How do you mean?"

"It's a poem by Rudyard Kipling. It's something every detective ought to know by heart. I learnt it when I was a boy. And it goes like this ...

I keep six honest serving-men
(They taught me all I knew);
Their names are What and Why and When
And How and Where and Who.

Sort out the first five, and we'll arrive at number 6."

"If we've got to do all that, we'd better get on with it, hadn't we, guv?" grinned Copper.

Sergeant Fletcher appeared in the library doorway. "I've told SOCO what you want, sir, and I managed to stop Dr. Livermore before he left. He's on his way back, but I should tell you, he's not a happy man."

"No," replied Constable wryly, "I had an idea he might not be. So in the interests of the good doctor's blood pressure, I think we perhaps ought to make ourselves scarce. Back to the billiard room, gentlemen."

Chapter 3

"What next, then, guv?" asked Dave Copper. "Where do you want to start on that list of yours?"

Andy Constable thought for a moment. "Let's be counter-intuitive and start at the end with the 'who'. Fletcher, I think you're best placed to help us out here. We know who's dead, so who else have we got in and around the case? For a start, who was in the house when it happened?"

"That's actually not quite as easy as it sounds, sir," said Sergeant Fletcher, reaching into a pocket for his notebook. "You've got the people who live in the house, but there were some visitors last night as well, so it's a bit complicated."

"Well, you'd better make it as simple as you can, since Copper here is going to be noting it all down. That's right, isn't it, sergeant?"

"Pen at the ready, sir," said Copper, hastily suiting the action to the word.

"So, let's start with who lives here. I'm assuming that butler chap is resident, since he looks as if they built the house around him."

"That's right, sir. Mr. Pelham."

"And he spoke of 'her ladyship', so I'm guessing there's a wife."

"Yes, sir. Lady Effingham was here yesterday evening. I believe there was some sort of dinner party planned, but of course that never came to anything."

"So who else? Any other family? Guests?"

"There's a nephew, sir. A Mr. ..." Fletcher checked his notes. "... Booker-Gresham, sir.

Apparently he's staying in the house at the moment. And there was a lady who was here for dinner ... a Mrs. Baverstock. She'd arrived about a quarter of an hour or so before the shooting."

"Is that it? This is a pretty big house. I imagine you're not going to tell me that Lady Effingham does all her own cooking and cleaning."

"No, sir. There's a housekeeper, Mrs. Carruthers. She does the cooking. And she's got her own rooms here as well, I gather."

"What about this gardener chap you mentioned ... the one who helped out with D.I. Warner?"

"Old Mr. Diggory? Oh, he lives on the estate, sir, in one of the lodges, I think, but he wasn't here in the house last night."

"Well, nevertheless, put him on the list, Copper," instructed Constable. "You never know, he may be able to tell us something useful about the set-up here. How many's that so far?"

"Six, guv."

"I'm afraid that's not all, sir," continued Fletcher apologetically. "There are a couple of others – well, they weren't actually in the house at the time, but they were about."

"This presumably is the complicated bit, sergeant," sighed Constable. "Care to explain?"

"There's a lady called Mrs. Wadsworth, sir, who called just before dinner, I gather. I don't think she was invited for the meal, and Mr. Pelham was a bit evasive about her, so I don't quite know what's going on there. But apparently she was gone before it all kicked off."

"Intriguing," remarked the inspector. "Well, we shall just have to *cherchez* that particular *femme* in due course. Next?"

"There were two gentlemen who turned up at the house just after the shooting, sir," reported Fletcher. "They were both involved with Sir Richard by way of his horse-racing business. Mr. Worcester, who I think was his business partner, and Mr. Elliott."

"Not Owen Elliott?" interjected Copper.

"Actually, yes."

Constable raised a quizzical eyebrow in Copper's direction. "You know him, sergeant?"

"Not personally, no, guv. But if it's the one I'm thinking of, he was the jockey who rode the winning horse in the 5000 Guineas, that day I went to the races. You remember, 'Last Edition'. Oh!" Copper stopped in sudden realisation. "Which ..."

"Which has very sadly just died," said Constable, picking up the thought. "Unfortunate coincidence, do we think? That would probably have been a very valuable animal. Well, let's not get ahead of ourselves. Fletcher, have you got contact details for all these people?"

"I have, sir."

The inspector reached a decision. "Look, why don't you let Sergeant Copper have all that? Then I'm sure you'll be wanting to get back to your own station instead of feeling, as you probably do, like something of a third wheel on the bike. I dare say you'll have plenty to keep you occupied on your own patch, particularly with D.I. Warner out of commission. And I expect you'll want to check up on him while you're about it. So leave a couple of Uniform sloshing about, and we'll take it from here." The dismissal, if unmistakeably couched, was at least considerately expressed. Constable consulted his watch. "Right, Copper, you note all that down, and then, as it's coming up to eleven o'clock, I think we'd better take up Mr. Pelham's suggestion and join Lady Effingham for coffee. It'll give us a chance to offer our condolences to the family and make a start on finding out what's what."

With the murmur of voices fading behind him, Andy Constable stepped out into the hall of the house. He looked up to where the light was filtering down from a timbered lantern glazed in the rich dense colours of high Victoriana. The stained glass portrayed mournful maidens standing beneath willow trees in a landscape backed by misty mountains, while knights with noble countenances and gleaming armour leaned down from high-stepping steeds to offer chivalric assistance. Everywhere in the hall below was the gleam of polished dark wood, the glint of multicoloured mosaic, the intricate patterning of terracotta tiling, and the opulence of oriental carpets. Marble busts gazed from pedestals. Between frescoed scenes of vaguely Arthurian legend, a panoply of medieval weaponry adorned the walls.

"I'm off, sir. And thank you." With a tone of something like relief in his voice, Sergeant Fletcher passed Constable and headed for the front door, as Dave Copper came to stand alongside his superior.

"So, back to just the old team then, guv." Copper joined the inspector in his perusal of their surroundings. "Bit of a mausoleum, this, isn't it, guv? Who on earth would want to live in a place like this?"

"A Victorian gentleman with impeccable taste, and a great deal of money to allow him to indulge it," came the slightly unexpected reply. "This is something of a Burges masterpiece."

"A what, sir?"

"William Burges, Copper," explained Constable patiently. "Another gap in your education I'm going to have to address, obviously. The man was the high priest of Victorian architecture and design. If you were building a house in eighteen-hundred-and-something, Burges was the man you called on to design it. Interiors too. No more of that nasty old Napoleonic classical style, all pillars and scrolls and sphinxes. This was how the masters of the British Empire expressed their ambition to rule the world. I grant you, it's not exactly what you'd want now in your average suburban semi, but for the great and the good of the time, this was cutting edge."

"All a bit gloomy for me, guv," replied Copper. "Give me a nice bit of Swedish flat-pack any day."

"And back down to earth with a bump we come," smiled Constable in resignation. "Well, enough about the rights and wrongs of house design. We have other wrongs to investigate. I take it you now know all there is to know about all the people we'll need to talk to."

"Yes, sir." Copper displayed his notebook, pages filled with cramped writing. "Fistfulls. I think I can make sense of it all."

"Good. Then we shall begin."

At that moment, a door covered in maroon baize and dotted with a pattern of brass studs opened next to the foot of the stairs, and the butler appeared, in his hands a tray bearing a silver coffee pot and cream jug together with two cups and saucers.

"Ah, Mr. Pelham," said Constable. "Just the man I need."

"How may I help you, sir?"

"We were wondering where we might find Lady Effingham."

"Her ladyship is in the morning room with Master James, sir. I'm just on my way there now, so if you would like to follow me ..." Pelham paused in front of the door next to the billiard room. "By the way, sir, it's Lady Olivia. As the daughter of an earl, her ladyship has the title in her own right. Before her marriage, she was Lady Olivia Stryde. Forgive me if I seem pedantic, sir, but I know that you police gentlemen like to have everything precisely correct."

"Indeed we do, Mr. Pelham," replied Constable, as Copper did his best to stifle a grin. "Thank you for that. And sergeant, instead of just standing there doing nothing with that silly look on your face, perhaps you'd like to get the door for Mr. Pelham."

"The gentlemen from the police, my lady," announced Pelham, as he entered the room and placed the coffee tray on a table beside the sofa.

The woman seated on the sofa rose and turned to greet the officers. Striking if not beautiful, she looked to be in her late fifties, with faded blonde hair drawn back into an elegant chignon. She wore black, a day dress relieved with touches of white at the wrist, with a single strand of pearls at her throat, and her almost unlined face bore the barest minimum of foundation and lipstick. She advanced on the inspector with a calm faint smile.

"Good morning, my lady," said Constable, taking his cue from the butler. "My name is Detective Inspector Constable. I've just taken over the conduct of this case from my colleague D.I. Warner, who as you know was unfortunately injured this morning."

"Ah yes." The smile took on a hint of apology. "Poor Mr. Warner. I'm afraid I shall have to speak very severely to Punter."

"Punter, madam?"

"My horse, inspector."

"Oh. Of course." Constable stepped aside to reveal Dave Copper, who had been standing behind him. "And I shall be assisted by my colleague here, Detective Sergeant Copper."

Lady Olivia's smile broadened. "Then I shall feel that I am in the best of hands. Good morning, Mr. Copper. I think you must have been promoted since we last met."

Constable was taken aback. "You ... you know Copper?"

"I wouldn't go so far as to say that, sir," protested the sergeant.

"Mr. Copper came to my father's house to take statements after we'd had a burglary," explained Lady Olivia. "I'd happened to be there that weekend."

"Copper ...?" Constable turned to his junior for clarification.

"The art thefts from the country houses, sir. I was sent as part of the team to Lord Warke's place. I'm surprised you remember me, my lady."

"My father always taught me, never forget a face or a name," said Lady Olivia. "But do, please, sit down, Mr. Constable." She waved to another sofa facing her own. "Sheba, move over." She issued a brisk instruction to the elderly golden retriever lying at her feet, which lazily rose, moved to the rug in front of the fireplace, and slumped back down with a profound sigh. "And I'm sure you would like some coffee. Pelham, would you please bring two further cups for the inspector and the sergeant."

"That really isn't necessary, my lady," said Constable, seating himself. "We don't wish to intrude any more than we have to at what must be a very difficult time for you. And please, let me offer my condolences on your loss. But I'm afraid I do have to ask you some questions."

"Of course," said Lady Olivia, accepting the coffee cup which Pelham handed her. Her face grew solemn. "The whole business is very unfortunate."

Constable blinked slightly at the choice of words. "I hope you won't object if Sergeant Copper makes some notes. And I apologise if I'm asking questions which you may have been asked before, but I have to bring myself up-to-date with the situation." A calm nod of acquiescence was the response. "Sir Richard Effingham was your husband?"

"Yes. We have been married for thirty-six

years."

"And would this be your son?" Constable turned to the dark-haired man in his thirties who sat, hitherto silent, in an armchair in the window recess.

"No. This is James, my nephew. Richard and I had no children."

"I see. Now, I need to establish some facts concerning yesterday evening. Can you tell me exactly when and where you last saw your husband?"

"It was around five past eight last night, inspector, in the drawing room. That's the equivalent room to this one, on the other side of the hall," explained Lady Olivia in reply to Constable's enquiring look. "Richard and I were having a drink in there as usual with James before dinner. But then Pelham came in to say that my husband had a visitor, so of course Richard excused himself to go out to attend to them."

"Did Mr. Pelham say who it was?"

"No, he didn't."

Constable swivelled in his seat to seek confirmation from the butler, but Pelham, after handing a cup of coffee to James, had faded unobtrusively from the room.

"I thought it might have been Julia Baverstock," continued Lady Olivia. "She'd been invited to dinner, but she didn't arrive until about five minutes after that. But Richard did have various people calling on him at various times, often in conjunction with the business, which I don't concern myself with, so I really thought no more about it. So the last I saw of Richard was when he left the room."

"And after that? Did you remain in the drawing room?"

"Yes. Well, actually, no. I was there for a little while, but then I went up to my room about a quarter of an hour later because I wanted to fetch a handkerchief."

"Leaving your guests alone?"

"Julia? Yes. James had already gone up to change. And it was only a little while later that I heard the shot from downstairs, so I came down and was told what had happened."

"Thank you, my lady. I think that's all very clear."

Lady Olivia stood abruptly. "Mr. Constable, would you think me awfully rude if I leave you? I quite suddenly feel rather tired, and I think I'd like to go and lie down."

The inspector got to his feet. "Of course ... by all means. This must have all come as a terrible shock. I'm sure we will be able to find you if there's anything further we need to ask."

"Thank you, inspector. Sergeant. Sheba, come along." With a gracious nod of her head, she walked steadily from the room, the dog ambling at her heels.

Andy Constable, after exchanging brief looks with Dave Copper, moved over to the other occupant of the room. "So, you were also here at the time, Mr. ...?"

"Booker-Gresham. James Booker-Gresham."

Constable took a seat in the armchair alongside the other man. "But do I understand correctly that you don't actually live in the house?"

"No. I live in London. I work in the City – I'm a trader with Bullings Bank."

"And you're Sir Richard and Lady Olivia's nephew?"

"That's right."

"Would that be on her ladyship's side or Sir Richard's?"

"Uncle Richard was my mother's brother. In fact, I suppose I'm the only relative he had, now that my ma's gone. There were just the two of them, you see, brother and sister, and I'm an only child."

A thought struck Constable. "Would that make you Sir Richard's heir?"

James smiled. "Do you know, I've never even thought about that, inspector. I suppose it might. It would all depend on his will, wouldn't it?"

"And the title. Sir Richard was a baronet, wasn't he? Will you be inheriting that?"

"That, definitely not. It doesn't descend through the female line, unfortunately." James shook his head regretfully. "Shame, really. It might have done me some good. There's lots of City firms who like to have a title somewhere about the place. Looks good on the letterhead. But no, it's not going to be 'Sir James'."

Constable reflected for a moment. "Can we come back to the details of yesterday evening?" he said. "By the way, how did you come to be in the house if you aren't resident here?"

"Oh, that's easy. Uncle Richard had asked me down to stay for a week. He did that once or twice a year after my parents died."

"And you were in the drawing room before dinner with Lady Olivia ...?"

"And that's the last time I saw my uncle. I didn't see him after he went to see his visitor just before dinner. In fact, I was up in my room when I heard a bang, so of course I came rushing down straight away, and Aunt Olivia told me what had happened."

"Tell me, sir – were you and your uncle on good terms?"

James seemed momentarily disconcerted by the question. "Of course. Why not?"

"No reason at all, sir," said Constable blandly. "But we always like to have a completely clear picture in a case of murder."

"Oh. I just wondered if somebody had said something, that's all. I mean, Uncle Richard and I had our ups and downs every so often, but who doesn't? You know, different generations and all that, but we got on fine. He wouldn't have asked me down to stay otherwise, would he?"

"I suppose not, sir. And perhaps you can tell me ... I didn't like to ask your aunt this question because I didn't want to cause her any further upset, but is there anyone you can think of who might wish your uncle harm?"

"No, inspector," said James. "Not a soul."

"In which case, sir, I think that will probably be all for the moment."

"Oh. Good." James put aside his half-drunk cup of coffee and stood. "Well, then, if you don't need me any more, I'll just ... I'll go and ... er ..." With a nervous smile, he made for the door and vanished into the hall.

"That was practically an escape, wasn't it, guv?" remarked Copper. "Our Mr. Booker-Gresham seems worried about something. Do we detect the sweaty palms of a murderer?"

"Far too early to start thinking in those terms, sergeant," replied Constable. "And far too obvious. I'm not leaping to any unwarranted conclusions until I know a great deal more about what happened last night and the people involved. So let us make a start."

Chapter 4

"Righty-ho, guv. So, where do we begin?"

As if on cue, Pelham materialised in the open doorway. "Oh, forgive me, gentlemen. I wasn't aware anyone was still here. I'd seen her ladyship and Master James leave, and I came to remove the coffee tray. I can easily come back later." He turned to leave.

Constable forestalled him. "No, don't do that, Mr. Pelham. In fact, you are just the person I need to speak to. Come in, close the door, and you can tell us what you know about what happened yesterday evening. Let's all sit down."

The butler shook his head. "Oh no, sir. Not in the drawing room. That wouldn't be right at all. But if you would like to follow me, I shall be happy to answer your questions in my pantry." Without waiting for any reply, Pelham collected the coffee cups from around the room, replaced them on the tray and, with an unhurried and stately gait, led the way along the hall and through the baize door through which he had appeared earlier. "If you would care to wait in here, inspector," he said, indicating the door to a small sitting room on the left as he pushed through a large heavy door which evidently led to the kitchen, returning empty-handed a few moments later. "Please sit down, gentlemen." The detectives took a seat on a faded brocade sofa while the butler lowered himself into a shabby leather armchair in front of the fireplace. "Now, how may I help you?"

"I'm hoping, Mr. Pelham, ..." began Constable.

"Just Pelham, sir," interrupted the butler.

The inspector smiled. "Since you don't work for me, Mr. Pelham, I think I'd prefer to err on the side of politeness, if you don't mind."

Pelham inclined his head. "As you wish, sir."

"And I'm sure it's not just Pelham, is it?" went on Constable. "I'm sure you have further names, which no doubt Sergeant Copper is just about to note down."

"Of course, sir." Copper attempted to make the hasty riffle of paper as unobtrusive as possible.

"It's Edward John Pelham, sergeant."

"Thank you, sir. And I understand you are resident at Effingham Hall?"

"Yes, sergeant. I have a modest apartment in the old servants' quarters up in the attics, and of course my small pantry here."

Constable resumed the questioning. "Would I be right in assuming that you have worked here for some time, Mr. Pelham?"

"Gracious, yes, sir," replied Pelham. He smiled in fond remembrance. "Probably more years than I care to remember. I've been with the family since Sir Richard's father was alive. A fine old gentleman, Sir Arthur, and a stickler for tradition. I came here as a second footman, in the days when there were such things. All very different in these days, of course."

"And I would imagine that you would be more familiar than anyone else about events in the house?"

"Indeed, sir. There's not much that goes on in this house that gets past me."

"So, tell me about yesterday. We need to

build up as complete a picture as we can of what happened. Anything unusual – that sort of thing."

"You mean, over and above the fact of Sir Richard's murder, sir?" Pelham sounded quite frosty.

"Quite." The inspector was apologetic. "I was thinking more of earlier in the day – anything that might have disrupted the normal routine of the house. Anything that might give us an inkling of what led up to later events."

The butler reflected for a moment. "As far as I recall, sir, the only thing which disrupted my usual routine was the fact that Master James failed to appear for luncheon, without a word to anybody. Not that that isn't just like him. But I thought it was most discourteous to Mrs. Carruthers, who had taken the trouble to prepare a particularly good cheese soufflé. Which, of course, could have been ruined."

"Did the family lunch at home most days?"

"Yes, sir. Except when Sir Richard was up at the stables, which hasn't been so frequent of late, or when he was away for the day at a race meeting, of course. But when Master James comes to stay, the family always lunches at home. And I have to say, Sir Richard was furious at Master James's absence. He won't stand for rudeness, you see, especially when it puts the staff out. Quite old-fashioned like that, he was."

"But obviously Mr. Booker-Gresham reappeared at some point."

"He did, sir. And if he'd only parked his car in the usual place, he might have avoided some of the unpleasantness."

The inspector's attention was alerted. "Unpleasantness? What do you mean, exactly?"

"The confrontation, if you can call it that, with Sir Richard, sir. You see, Master James came back at almost exactly half past two ..."

"How can you be so precise, Mr. Pelham?" broke in Copper, busily noting details.

"Because, sergeant, Sir Richard was going out of the front door for his usual afternoon walk, and he came face to face with Master James who had just parked his car at the foot of the steps."

"And you're certain of the exact time?" persisted Copper.

"I am, sir, and for two reasons. Firstly, because I happened to be by as the clock in the hall was striking, and secondly, because Sir Richard was very much a creature of habit. He would always go out on the stroke of 2.30, taking his stick and the dog. Now if Master James had only been a little more observant on his visits, he would have known that, but of course, young people pay so little attention to their elders these days." A sigh of regret.

"You said something about unpleasantness," resumed Constable. "What happened?"

"Oh, I don't mean anything in the way of an argument, sir," said Pelham hastily. "Sir Richard would never have done such a thing with me there. As I say, he was quite old-fashioned – *'pas devant les domestiques'*, and all that. But he did say that he would be speaking to Master James later, and from the look on his face, I don't think the young man liked the sound of that. Anyway, he went back down the steps to his car and drove it off round the house to park it, I suppose. And Sir Richard stood there for a few moments and then carried on."

"So Sir Richard was alone when he went for his walk?"

"No, inspector. Because as Master James drove away, Mrs. Baverstock drove up. I could see her through the window by the front door."

"The lady who came to dinner?" Constable sought to confirm.

"That's correct, sir, although I wasn't aware until later that she had been invited. But she was getting out of her car just as Sir Richard was going down the steps towards the west terrace. And they were talking together as they went round the corner of the house."

"Do you know when Sir Richard returned?"

"He came back at about half past four, sir."

"On his own?"

"Certainly, sir. Mrs. Baverstock had left by then – at least, her car was gone, but I'm afraid I can't tell you when. But just as Sir Richard was coming in through the front door, Mr. Worcester drove up."

"Mr. Worcester?" Constable looked to Copper for elucidation.

"The business partner of Sir Richard, sir, I believe. We've got him on our list."

"Good. So, you were saying that this Mr. Worcester arrived ...?"

"Indeed, sir. It was one of those days for comings and goings. But it isn't as if he wasn't expected. You see, Sir Richard had asked me to call

Mr. Worcester that morning and ask him to come over. And then when Mr. Worcester arrived, Sir Richard said something like 'Ah, I want to see you – there's something we've got to sort out', and the two gentlemen went through to the library."

"Leaving you to take care of the dog and so on?" smiled Constable.

"Well, no sir, not on this occasion," said Pelham "I usually manage to keep an eye cocked for Sir Richard's return, and he would normally hand me his stick and the dog's lead, and I would take Sheba through to the kitchen for a drink and a little treat. Not strictly according to the rules, I know, but Sheba's no trouble, and Mrs. Carruthers doesn't really mind, although she pretends to. But there are always a few titbits put aside from lunch." A fond smile.

"But you say that yesterday was different?"

"Yes, sir. And now I come to think of it, it's a little odd. Because Sir Richard went on through, still with Sheba and carrying his stick, instead of giving it to me to replace in the hall stand. And yet that is where it was found after the murder."

"Probably put it back himself later," put in Copper reasonably.

"Well, anything odd is the sort of thing that's worth pursuing, Mr. Pelham," said Constable, "so thank you for that. So, that's two callers to the house so far. Any others?"

"Well, sir." Pelham looked slightly uneasy. "There was a telephone call from Mrs. Wadsworth at about five past seven. I took it here in the hall, and I put it though to Sir Richard in the library. Oh, and that was just after the call from Mr. Elliott. I almost forgot to mention that."

"Did either of them say why they wanted to speak to Sir Richard?"

"No, sir, and of course, it would not be proper for me to enquire."

"So you would have no idea what would be the nature of these telephone calls? You didn't happen to overhear anything as you put them through?" Constable was hoping against hope that natural human curiosity might have played a part.

"Certainly not, sir." Pelham's tone was highly disapproving of the suggestion.

"Well, then," said the inspector, feeling slightly chastened, "we'll move on. What can you tell us about visitors to the house?"

The unease returned. "Mrs. Wadsworth did in fact come to the house a little later, sir. I let her in at five past eight and took her through to the library."

"Was Sir Richard still there?"

"No, sir. That was the time when the family had gathered in the drawing room for drinks prior to dinner, and Sir Richard was there. But I thought it best to show Mrs. Wadsworth through to the library."

"Indeed?" Constable waited, eyebrows raised invitingly, for an explanation.

"Yes, sir." Pelham kept his face completely impassive. "Mrs. Wadsworth didn't usually come to the house when Lady Olivia was at home, but of course, it wouldn't be up to me to say why. But then I went to the drawing room to tell Sir Richard that he had a visitor."

"Did you tell him who it was?"

"I thought it wisest not to, sir."

"And you then continued serving drinks, I presume?"

"Oh no, sir. I never had anything to do with the drinks before dinner."

"So you didn't remain in the drawing room?"

"No, sir. I returned here to my pantry."

"And what about the period after Mrs. Wadsworth arrived?"

"I answered the bell at the front door about five minutes later – that was Mrs. Baverstock, who I understood had been invited to join the family for dinner."

"Had you been aware of that, Mr. Pelham?"

"I believe Mrs. Carruthers had been informed by her ladyship during the course of the afternoon, sir. So naturally I showed Mrs. Baverstock into the drawing room to join her ladyship and Master James."

"Tell me, did you notice anything in particular about the manner of any of the visitors to the house?" Pelham looked surprised at the inspector's question. "I'm trying to gather whether any of them might have given any indication of tension between themselves and Sir Richard."

"I really couldn't say, sir," replied Pelham. "In any case, it would have been most improper for me to have noticed anything of the kind."

Constable sighed inwardly at the traditional reticence of the perfect butler. "And after Mrs. Baverstock's arrival ...?"

"I came back to the kitchen to advise Mrs.

Carruthers that the dinner party was assembled and to see if I could assist her in any way with the final preparations for the meal, sir. And I was just getting ready to announce dinner when I heard the shot."

"At what time was that? Can you recall?

"Oh yes, sir. Precisely. You see, dinner is always served at 8.30 exactly – Sir Richard was always insistent on punctuality – so I always leave the kitchen at 8.27 by the clock there to get to the drawing room at 8.28."

"Now, this is extremely important, Mr. Pelham. Can you tell us the exact sequence of events after that?"

"Yes, inspector. I heard a shot from the library, so I rushed in. The room was in virtual darkness – only the small desk lamp was on – so I turned on the lights, and there was the Master, dead."

"Alone? What about Mrs. Wadsworth?"

"There was no sign of her, sir. And the room was full of the smell of gas ..."

"Gas?" queried Constable in astonishment. "What, you mean some sort of poisonous fumes?"

"Oh no, sir. Ordinary domestic gas. So of course I switched it off, opened all the windows, and went back out into the hall. Her ladyship and Master James were just coming downstairs, and Mrs. Baverstock was in the drawing room doorway. I explained what I had found – of course, everyone seemed shocked and upset, so I suggested that they stay in the drawing room, and then I went to telephone the police straight away."

"That ties in with what Sergeant Fletcher told

us, sir," reported Copper. "He told us the call was logged at 8.29pm."

"So after that?" asked Constable.

"As soon as I put down the phone it rang again, sir. I thought it must be the police calling back to confirm the incident, but actually it was Mr. Worcester. Of course, I told him what had happened, and he said he would come straight over. And in fact, he arrived at the same time as the police car."

"At which point I think we can pick up the narrative from our local colleagues," concluded Constable. "That's if there's nothing more you can tell us."

"Nothing that is germane to your enquiries, sir."

"Hmmm." The inspector did not sound wholly convinced. He rose to his feet. "Very well, Mr. Pelham. Well, we won't keep you any longer. I dare say you have a considerable amount to get on with. As have we, Copper, so I suggest we do so." He led the way out of the service quarters and back into the hall.

"Any preference, guv?" enquired Copper as the two detectives stood beneath the ornately-branching brass chandelier at the foot of the stairs. He brandished his notebook. "I'm starting to get a ton of stuff in here, but at the moment it seems like more questions than answers."

"The only way we shall get answers is to put those questions to the people concerned," retorted Constable reasonably. "Who's next on the list?"

Copper consulted his notes and pondered for a moment. "Hold on a second, guv." He pulled out his phone and spent several moments tapping at the screen. "Can I make a suggestion, sir?"

"All helpful suggestions gratefully received."

"How about we start with the people who were actually on the scene when the shot was heard, which I'm assuming was the crucial moment, and then work our way outwards?"

"Sounds sensible. Go on."

"There's this Mrs. Baverstock, sir." He broke off. "I'm sure I know that name from somewhere. Can't think where ..." He shrugged. "Anyway, she was in the drawing room when the big bang happened, so she's the obvious next candidate, and I've got her address here. She lives in a house up on the downs, which as it happens is sort of on the way to the stables where Sir Richard trained his horses, so I'm guessing we'd be likely to find Mr. Worcester there. He got here just after it all happened, plus we ought to be able to get a lot of useful background on who and what. And then if we came back in a big loop, it would bring us round to Knaggs End village, which is where our mystery woman Mrs. Wadsworth lives. Although, to be honest, guv, I don't actually think there's a great deal of mystery about her. Other than where she went last night and when. I bet you'll be wanting to know that. How does that sound?"

Constable smiled. "Who needs sat nav when you have an efficient sergeant to do all the hard work of navigation?" he remarked approvingly. "Anyway, that electronic woman's voice drives me mad. But this sounds very much like one of your cunning plans, and I don't think I can fault it. As long as you don't get us lost up these back lanes."

"Don't worry, guv," grinned Copper. "I've got a sat nav app on my phone as well. I've worked it all out. No chance of sending us off in the wrong direction."

"I shall very conveniently forget some of the blind alleys you've tried to lead us up on previous cases!" laughed Constable.

At that moment, a figure clad in pale blue overalls, face half covered by a surgical mask, emerged from the library. "Oh, good morning, sir. I didn't know you were involved with this case." The mask was removed.

The inspector's face lit up in a smile of recognition. "Sergeant Singleton! This is an unexpected pleasure. I think the last time we met was at the Queen's Theatre, wasn't it? I had no idea you were here working in this neck of the woods."

"Transferred across, sir." The Scene Of Crime Officer pulled back her hood and shook her blonde hair loose. "Not quite a promotion, but the next best thing. And I'm enjoying the change of scenery."

"Although not exactly a change of responsibility," said Constable. "So, do you have anything particularly interesting to report thus far?"

"Actually, sir, quite a few things, but the team's still working, so we may well turn up more stuff for you before we're finished. Would you like a progress report?"

Constable considered. "On reflection, no. Copper and I ... you remember Copper, don't you?"

"Oh yes, sir. Very well." The two sergeants exchanged nods and smiles, Singleton's appearing to contain just a little extra sparkle.

"We were just off to pursue other avenues, so why don't we let you compile your complete dossier and we'll have it all in one lump instead of piecemeal."

"Fine by me, sir."

"In which case, Copper, let's go – out to the car. We'll see if this cunning plan of yours works in practice."

Chapter 5

"Guv," said Dave Copper, as the car began the climb up and out of the valley of Knaggs End.

"Mmm?" responded Andy Constable absently, concentrating on navigating around a tractor and trailer laden with large rolls of fodder.

"What exactly is a baronet?"

"I'm surprised at you, sergeant," replied Constable. "As the man who consorts with earls and their daughters, I should have thought you'd be totally conversant with the ins and outs of the English nobility."

"I must have been off school the day they covered that. So I suppose that lets me in for one of my usual instructive seminars, sir," said Copper resignedly.

"Don't complain, sergeant. You ask a question, you have to put up with the answer. Personally, I'd have thought you'd have learnt by now." A smiling Constable settled to his theme. "A baronetcy is the lowest level of nobility. It's a sort of hereditary knighthood. Hence the 'Sir'. But unlike an ordinary knighthood, it carries on down the family. So if, god forbid, the sovereign took it into their head to make you a knight ..."

"Actually, guv, I quite like the sound of that," grinned the younger man. "'Sir David Copper' has got a pretty good ring to it, don't you reckon?"

"As I said, god forbid! But in the unlikely event of this lunatic scenario coming about, your 'Sir' would expire when you do. A baronet, on the other hand, can pass his title down."

"So if I became 'Sir Dave, Baronet' ..."

"And if you ever managed to persuade one of these poor girls you keep having these ephemeral relationships with to stick around long enough actually to marry you, and you had a son ..."

"... he'd end up as 'Sir Dave Junior' or whatever."

Constable sighed. "Quite. Which is why, as soon as we get back to the station, I shall lose no time in firing off an email to the Palace recommending that they never consider doing any such thing! The prospect of an ermine-clad Copper is too appalling to contemplate. Now, enough of these flights of fancy. Let's concentrate on getting to our next port of call."

Copper checked his phone. "In which case, guv, you'd better turn left here."

Julia Baverstock's house lay behind high sheltering hedges on the windswept fringe of the downs. As Constable's car crunched to a halt on the gravel sweep in front of the door, he reflected that there appeared to be no shortage of money here. A fountain played in the centre of a tiny immaculate knot garden in the centre of the drive, while manicured lawns ran on either side up to a house which, although clearly of modern construction and modest in size, was a flawless evocation of the Georgian style.

"Worth a pretty penny, guv, this place," remarked Copper as the detectives climbed from the car. "Whatever Mrs. Baverstock does, I reckon it pays well." He paused. "You know, I swear that name rings a bell."

"Well, instead of standing there scratching your head, why don't you ring the bell in practice?" replied Constable. "Then we shall have to wonder no longer."

The woman who answered the door was elegant and well-groomed and, Constable estimated, somewhere in her late forties. A sage-green long-sleeved silk blouse was teamed with a slim tailored black skirt and black patent court shoes. Her glossy dark hair just brushed her shoulders. A ring set with what appeared to be a significant emerald was her only jewellery.

"Yes?"

"Mrs. Julia Baverstock? I'm Detective Inspector Constable – this is Detective Sergeant Copper." The two officers showed their credentials. "We're making enquiries into the death of Sir Richard Effingham. May we come in?"

"Of course." Julia stepped back to allow the detectives to enter, and then led the way across the hall towards the back of the house. "I've been expecting somebody. The inspector who came to Richard's house last night told me that he would be in touch," she said over her shoulder, as she entered a large and comfortable sitting room with spectacular views over rolling countryside. "Do please sit down." She waved to a large chintz-covered sofa and seated herself in an armchair alongside the fireplace. "Actually, I expected it would be the same gentleman."

"I'm afraid Inspector Warner is no longer available to handle the case," said Constable. "He had something of a *contretemps* with Lady

Effingham's horse, so I've had to take over."

"Oh dear." Julia attempted to stifle a smile. "No, it's not really funny. But Punter can be somewhat temperamental if you don't treat him with the right degree of respect. Some hunters can be like that. But I suspect you probably have other matters you'd rather ask me about."

"Yes, Mrs. Baverstock," agreed Constable. "We haven't really come here to talk about horses."

"I'm afraid you may have to," said Julia. "However ..." She took a breath. "How can I help you?"

"I suppose we had better start with the basics. You are Julia Baverstock. Mrs." A nod in confirmation. "Is there a Mr. Baverstock?"

"Not for several years, inspector. My late husband died in an industrial accident. He was crushed to death by a roll of paper."

"I beg your pardon?" Constable sounded bewildered.

"At the printing works he owned," explained Julia. "Some of the machinery malfunctioned, and a roll of paper fell where he happened to be standing. He died immediately."

"Oh. I'm sorry. I had no idea."

"There's no reason why you should, inspector. And, as I say, it's some years ago now, and I think you're probably more concerned with more recent events."

"Indeed." Constable accepted the gentle hint to return to the matter in hand. "And I'm hoping you may be able to give us some information, as you were on the scene yesterday at the time of the unfortunate death of Sir Richard Effingham."

"I think you mean 'murder', don't you, inspector?" Julia was obviously not a woman to beat about the bush.

"I do, Mrs. Baverstock. So perhaps we can begin by asking how you knew Sir Richard?"

"Oh, in many ways. We'd known each other for years. He was a great friend of my husband's. They were at school together. My husband was some years older than me," she added in response to the inspector's enquiring glance. "And then there were the books, naturally."

"I don't follow. Which books would these be?"

"Richard's books, of course." The uncomprehending look on Constable's face encouraged Julia to continue. "I'm sorry, inspector – I thought you would have known."

"I'm beginning to realise that, having come into this case part-way through, I'm rather playing catch-up with some of the background, Mrs. Baverstock," said Constable ruefully. "Perhaps you'd be good enough to fill me in."

"Richard wrote whodunnits, inspector. Murder mysteries – detective novels – call it what you will. You might have come across them, although they're probably not the sort of thing a professional like yourself would be caught dead reading, but they are still quite popular with the general public. 'Murder For The Defence' is one of his best-known. No?" Head-shaking from the two police officers. "He wrote them, they were initially printed on my husband's company's presses, and of course I published them through my publishing company. As it happens, there is a new one due out soon – 'Bell, Book, and Murder'. In fact, Richard's death may well have a positive effect on sales, if that doesn't make me sound too heartless."

"I wasn't aware that you were a publisher, Mrs. Baverstock. And I have to say that I'm afraid I'd never heard Sir Richard's name before I became involved in this investigation."

"Oh, he didn't write under his own name. I suspect that some of the circles he moved in might have looked down on his particular literary genre. No, he wrote under the name of Jolyon Booker – 'Jolyon' was one of his middle names, and I believe he took the 'Booker' from his sister's married name. But of course, the books were merely a sideline. Richard's first love was always racing and the horses he trained. That was the other link between us."

"Oh?"

"Yes. He trained my racehorse, 'Last Edition'." A cloud passed over Julia's face. "That is, until recent events."

Dave Copper snapped his fingers. "That's where I knew the name from!" he blurted, causing the other two to look at him in surprise. "Sorry, sir," he continued. "I did say I thought I knew Mrs. Baverstock's name, and it's just come to me. You were the owner of the horse I won some money on in the Five Thousand Guineas."

"Congratulations, sergeant," said Julia. "Evidently we both made something of a killing that day." She gave a slightly wan smile. "An unfortunate choice of words, since he had to be put down just at the peak of his career. But sadly, things like that can happen in the horse-racing world."

"I imagine you would have been rather upset," said Constable. "Particularly as I gather from my sergeant here that 'Last Edition' was probably a very valuable animal."

"As you say, inspector. We had plans to retire him from racing and send him to stud. But ..." A rueful shrug. "Not everything works out as you intend."

"Perhaps we should return to the events of yesterday," said Constable. "And yesterday evening in particular."

A meaningful throat-clearing came from Sergeant Copper at his side. "Although I have a note, sir, that Mrs. Baverstock was on the premises earlier in the day. Mr. Pelham did mention ..."

"Indeed he did, sergeant. And thank you for the reminder. So, Mrs. Baverstock, can you tell us what occasioned these two visits in one day?"

"It's perfectly simple, inspector," said Julia calmly. "One led on from the other. I needed to see Richard because I wanted to talk to him about 'Printer's Devil' – that's another horse I'm looking to buy. The breeding's good, but he's untried."

"So you were seeking Sir Richard's advice? And also with a view to having him train your new acquisition?"

"Well, that would be the natural assumption, wouldn't it, inspector? And we had a brief conversation, but Richard suggested that I might like to come to dinner so that we could discuss the matter in a more leisurely fashion. Of course, I accepted."

"So you returned to Effingham Hall later. And arrived when ...?"

Julia thought for a moment. "I got there about ten past eight, I suppose. Then I had a drink with Olivia and James in the drawing room."

"Sir Richard wasn't there at that point?"

"No. Olivia said something about him having gone to attend to a visitor in the library. So we just chatted about this and that."

"You didn't notice anything unusual about the atmosphere?"

"Not a thing, inspector. Although I have to say, I was rather preoccupied with thoughts of the horse."

"And you remained there all together in the drawing room?" asked Constable artlessly.

"Oh no, inspector. Both Olivia and James left the room at various times. They both went upstairs, I think. But I was certainly there when the shot came. I knew what it was at once. The sound of a shotgun is quite unmistakeable, even through a couple of closed doors. So I went out to the hall straight away, and Pelham was just coming out of the library. He told us what had happened, and of course Olivia wanted to go in there, but Pelham said that it would probably be best if nobody else went into the room until the police arrived, and he went to telephone immediately while I took Olivia into the drawing room. And that's where we stayed until the officers arrived."

*

"I noticed the trap you laid for the lady, guv,"

remarked Dave Copper as the detectives climbed back into the car.

"Yes," replied Andy Constable. "Although in backing up what Lady Olivia and James said about who was where and when, she has very inconveniently, as far as she is concerned, left herself with nobody who can confirm her own whereabouts in the period running up to the murder. Which may or may not be significant. After all, Pelham said she was in the drawing room immediately after the shot, so I don't see how she could have been in two places at once. Well, it's all material for your steadily-increasing dossier."

"I may need another notebook if it goes on like this, guv," grinned Copper. "Off to the next one, is it?"

"It is. So get your phone out, and kindly resist the temptation to give the directions in an annoying electronic voice."

"I could do Popeye, sir." A growl from the inspector led to a brisk tapping of Copper's phone screen. "Okay, guv. It's turn right out of the drive ..."

The Effingham establishment lay on one of the highest parts of the downs. An unostentatious gateway, flanked by a pair of modest signs featuring a horse's profile intertwined with a stylised 'E', was the only indication of its existence, and beyond a cattle grid, a gravelled drive led the short distance towards a surprisingly domestic-looking bungalow just within the property, before continuing in the direction of a belt of trees which, Constable assumed, sheltered the main group of buildings. A solitary horse grazed calmly in a distant corner of one of the flanking fields. Outside the bungalow, a metallic grey Mercedes was parked.

"Doesn't look much, guv," commented Copper as the car turned in and parked alongside the Mercedes outside a front door simply labelled 'Office'. "I got the impression that there was loads of money sloshing around horse-racing."

"Let's go and find out," said Constable, and led the way through the door. "Hello," he called. "Is there anyone here?"

The man who emerged from one of the rooms leading off the hall was short and heavily-built, a fact which the expertly-tailored suit was unable to disguise. A jowly face with small quick darting eyes was topped by a bald crown fringed with short grey hair. "Can I help?" The cultivated voice somehow did not seem to go with the visual image.

"I'm looking for Mr. Simon Worcester."

"That's me."

"I'm Detective Inspector Constable, sir, and this is Detective Sergeant Copper." The officers presented their warrant cards.

"Ah. This business with Richard."

"Yes, sir. We are investigating Sir Richard Effingham's death, and we were hoping to ask you some questions."

"Of course, inspector. You'd better come through." He moved back into what was evidently his office, furnished in modern style with pale wood furniture and chrome-and-leather chairs of an unmistakeably Scandinavian origin. He settled himself at a desk strewn with papers, while the detectives took seats opposite. He reached for a glass on the desk. "Drink?"

"No thank you, sir. On duty, and all that."

"Oh. Right. Well, I will, if you don't mind." Simon pulled open the top drawer of the desk and rummaged for a moment, before standing and producing a bottle of whisky from a drawer in a filing cabinet behind him. He splashed a measure into his glass. "What would you like to know?"

Constable smiled faintly. "Pretty much everything, sir, really. My colleague and I have been brought into the case in place of the original investigating officer, so we're still compiling as much background as we can." A glance towards Copper to ensure that the sergeant's notebook was at the ready. "I believe I'm right in saying that you and Sir Richard worked together."

"Yes. We were partners in the business."

"And was this a long-standing arrangement? I mean, had you known Sir Richard for a long time?"

"Oh, absolutely. Forever. Well, since we were at Eddie's together."

"'Eddie's', sir? How do you mean?"

"Sorry, inspector. Richard and I were both Old Edmundians. From St. Edmund's College. Founded by Henry VII, you know. Or perhaps you don't. The school was never quite as famous as its bigger rival down-river at Eton, but a very good establishment for all that. So yes, Richard and I first met at school, which must be fifty-odd years ago now." Simon shook his head. "Lord. Where do the years go?"

"And you've remained in contact in one way

or another ever since?"

"Not exactly, no. I went on up to university and then into the money business, whereas Richard had no need to. He had a ready-made career in his father's business. So we lost touch for a while. But then when Richard's father died and Richard took over, he made a few changes." Simon smiled. "Old Sir Arthur was a fine old gentleman, but he was somewhat stuck in the nineteenth century as far as running a business was concerned. Richard was rather like him in some ways – there wasn't a thing he didn't know about training horses, but he could never get on with the ins and outs of administration. And he and I happened to run into each other at an O.E.'s function – I think it may have been to celebrate the retirement of one of the masters who'd been there since god was a lad, or some such. It was twenty years or so ago, so I'm afraid the details are somewhat hazy, but the point was, we got chatting, and the upshot was that, as he couldn't stand paperwork and I was a money man, he offered to take me into the business to handle all the admin and the books. And here I am."

"A perfect example of the old boy network in practice, sir," said Constable.

"Exactly, inspector."

"Just as a matter of interest, Mr. Worcester, what happens to the business now? I'm presuming you and Sir Richard had some sort of formal arrangement ...?"

"There was a partnership agreement, yes. I can't remember the details exactly."

"If my memory serves me right, I believe that

there would normally be some sort of clause about the assets devolving on to the surviving partner in the event of the death of one of them, sir." Constable smiled self-deprecatingly. "I'm afraid my contract law is rather rusty."

"Yes ... yes, I think there was something of the sort."

"Which then brings us rather neatly to the present, Mr. Worcester, and the events of yesterday."

Simon's face took on a sad expression. "This is all terrible, inspector. Who on earth could have wanted to kill Richard?"

"That's a question I was hoping to ask you, sir. Now, since you were at Sir Richard's house yesterday ..."

"But not at the time he was killed, inspector. I didn't get there until afterwards, so I don't know that I can tell you much about what happened. In fact, if I hadn't phoned up, I wouldn't have known. But I called, it seems just after it happened, and Pelham told me there had been a shooting and that Richard was dead. I couldn't believe it. I got into my car and drove straight over – I don't really know why – I must have had some idea of being able to offer to help in some way. And I got there just as the police were arriving."

"So I understand, sir. But I also understand that you went to the house earlier in the day. I was wondering if that might have had any bearing on events."

Simon furrowed his brow. "I can't see how, inspector. I'd gone over because I'd needed to see

Richard because there was something I had to sort out with him – oh, nothing particularly significant, inspector. Just some paperwork that I wanted a signature on. So we spoke, and then I came away not long afterwards."

"And as far as you were aware, there was nothing in Sir Richard's manner to lead you to suspect any problems?"

Simon gave a small wry laugh. "Obviously you've never worked with horses, inspector. There are always problems. We get through them."

"I believe you had an unfortunate accident with one of your horses recently. Mrs. Baverstock's 'Last Edition', wasn't it? We've just come from speaking to her."

There was an increase in the air of unease. "But why ... I mean, what's she been telling you?"

"Nothing specific, sir, other than that the horse had to be put down."

"Yes, well, as you say, that was very sad. But as for Richard, no, as far as he and I were concerned, everything was perfectly normal."

"And you say that you can think of no reason why anyone would wish to do Sir Richard harm? Nobody with any sort of grudge against him? No feelings running high?"

"Feelings always run high in the horse-racing world," replied Simon. "It's that kind of business. But as for what anyone else might have been feeling, I really can't answer for that. You'll have to ask other people."

"Oh, don't worry, sir. We shall. We have quite a long list of people we're planning on talking to."

Constable made to get to his feet. "By the way, sir, my colleague and I were faintly surprised when we arrived that there seemed a distinct lack of horses and facilities for an establishment of this kind. I was given to understand that the Effingham stables were quite prominent in the horse-racing world."

Simon smiled. "We are, inspector. Please don't be fooled by this little house. This used to be a smallholding with a couple of fields, but we had the chance to buy them up, so we could increase the grazing and put in a new access road. The old one's up a very twisting lane – no good for anything other than a single horse-box. And I decided to use the bungalow as an office, to keep me away from all the hurly-burly of the stables. My flat's in Westchester, but this gives me somewhere to stay if I happen to be working particularly late. Like I said, I'm just the paper-pusher. But all the main facilities are up over the other side of the hill."

"Beyond the trees?"

"Yes. That's where we have the stable yard and the *manège* and the therapy pool and so on. And the gallops go down into the valley and back." Simon stood. "I could show you if you like."

"I'm sure that's not necessary, sir," answered Constable. "Fascinating as it might be, but we have rather more pressing needs. So I think that will be all for now, and we'll get in touch with you if there's anything more we need. We'll let you get back to your paperwork." He extended his hand in farewell, and the two detectives made their way back out to the car.

Chapter 6

"Thoughts, sergeant?" invited Andy Constable as he settled behind the wheel.

"A couple of things, sir," replied Dave Copper. "Something of a lack of straight answers to the questions regarding whether Sir Richard had any problems, either his own or with anybody else. And also on the matter of whether anybody else had a problem with Sir Richard that might give them a motive to kill him."

"My thinking exactly," said Constable. "I think there's more scope for digging." He switched on the car engine.

"You'll be wanting directions for our next digging site then, guv." Copper pulled his phone out of his pocket, gave a few taps to the screen, and perused the result. "Okay – according to Coppernav, we're back out of here, turn left, and then straight on for about a mile. That's just for starters."

"Remind me. This will take us to ...?"

"Mrs. Wadsworth, sir. Sarah Wadsworth."

Once back off the downs, the route led through a succession of tiny villages. Chocolate-box cottages with thatched roofs peeped shyly from behind luxuriant hedges, while substantial brick-built Georgian houses kept themselves to themselves, surrounded by high walls which allowed the merest glimpse of the property through intricately-wrought iron gates. At intervals, a yew-flanked church, modest in scale and featuring the flint-work characteristic of the area, stood in its own charmingly dishevelled graveyard, where the occasional bright splash of colour from freshly-laid flowers contrasted with the leisurely but relentless scramble of ivy over the tombs of long-departed parishioners. Eventually there appeared a roadside sign which welcomed visitors to Knaggs End and invited them to drive carefully through the village.

"It's the right turn just before the pub, sir," directed Copper. "Saddler's Lane. And we want 'Hilton House' – they don't seem to have house numbers round here."

The inspector drove the car on to the drive of a detached three-storey Edwardian house which exuded an air of comfortable prosperity. An immaculate front lawn was fringed by colourful flower beds, while an impressive willow tree drooped over the entrance to the drive. In front of the garage at the side of the house stood a small black sports car, its top down, its long bonnet hinting that power was not necessarily linked to size.

"Somebody else who's worth a pretty penny, guv," remarked Copper, taking in the scene.

"You'd probably be hard pressed to find many people round here who aren't," replied Constable. "It's that kind of area. So, let's see if we can discover what sort of woman the slightly mysterious Mrs. Wadsworth turns out to be." He climbed the steps to the front door and rang the bell.

"Yes, can I help?"

The detectives turned in surprise at the voice from behind them, as a woman appeared from around the side of the house. She looked to be in her late thirties, with long blonde hair casually tied back in a ponytail. She wore a light-coloured check shirt topped by a light waistcoat, jodhpurs, black leather riding boots with tan tops, while a riding hat swung by its chinstrap from one hand, the other carrying a riding crop. Her face was a classic oval, almost devoid of make-up save for a touch of lipstick, and a pair of enormous grey eyes gazed at her visitors enquiringly from beneath perfectly arched eyebrows. The accent was cut-glass.

"Would you be Mrs. Sarah Wadsworth?"

"Yes. What's this about? I was just on my way out."

"I'm sorry if this is a bad time, Mrs. Wadsworth, but I'm afraid we shall have to delay you," replied the inspector. He produced his warrant card and introduced himself. "May I take it you've heard about Sir Richard Effingham?"

"That he's dead? Yes, there was something on the radio this morning."

"And as we understand you were among his friends, we'd like to ask you some questions if we may."

"You'd better follow me, inspector," said Sarah. "Come round the back. Shamrock will have to wait."

"Do I take it that Shamrock is the name of your horse?" asked Constable, as Sarah casually discarded her riding equipment and sat in one of the wicker armchairs placed around a glass-topped table on the paved terrace overlooking the garden at the rear of the house, gesturing to the police officers to do likewise.

"It is," said Sarah. "I like to ride every

morning whenever I can. And today was too good to miss." She looked expectantly at Constable and waited.

"You visited Sir Richard yesterday shortly before his death," began the inspector without preamble. "When his body was discovered, you had apparently left the house. I was hoping you could fill in some details for me."

"There's nothing sinister, inspector, if that's what you're implying. I wished to speak to Richard, so I went to the house and did so. After we spoke, I left. It was a private matter."

Constable gave a wintery smile. "I'm afraid, Mrs. Wadsworth, that in a case of murder, very few things can be allowed to remain a private matter. Now, let me see if I can help you out by telling you what we already know. We've had a conversation with Mr. Pelham, Sir Richard's butler, who told us that you had telephoned Sir Richard earlier in the evening. He also told us at what time he admitted you to the house. But he was somewhat reticent on the subject of your visit. However, what he did let fall was the fact that you, as a rule, did not call at the house when Sir Richard's wife was on the premises. So, you were perhaps a friend of Sir Richard's rather than a friend of the family?"

"Yes." Sarah did not seem disposed to be any more forthcoming.

"Had you known him long?"

"About fifteen years."

"There was, I think, some considerable difference in your ages," said the inspector carefully.

"I'm not at all sure what you're implying by

that," responded Sarah in a slightly frosty tone. "Some men carry their years lightly. Richard could hold his own with men twenty years younger than himself. Some men of that age think they can keep up, but they are just deluded. I mean, Simon, for god's sake!" A laugh of derision.

Constable was alerted. "You mean Simon Worcester? Sorry, are you telling us that Mr. Worcester and you ...?"

"Simon? Oh god, no. He might have wanted to, but ... really, inspector, no."

"But in Sir Richard's case, yes? You were very happy in your friendship with him?"

"I suppose you might say so," said Sarah carefully.

"And how would you characterise this friendship?" persisted Constable. "Good friends? Extremely good friends? Intimate friends?"

Sarah gave a sigh of exasperation. "Yes, inspector, if you wish to put it that way, we were very close friends."

"To be blunt, you were his mistress?"

Sarah burst out into rather surprising laughter. "What a very bourgeois question! All right, inspector, if that's the word you like to use, you are correct. I was his mistress, or, at least, I was until recently."

"Until yesterday, are you saying? Was this in fact the reason for your visit to him? I think, Mrs. Wadsworth, that it would probably save us all a great deal of time if you would tell us the whole story."

Sarah sighed again. "Very well, inspector."

She pulled a slim gold case from a waistcoat inside pocket, extracted a cigarette and, after fruitlessly patting her other pockets, grimaced and replaced the cigarette in the case. "I've been meaning to give up anyway." She took a deep breath and seemed to be marshalling her thoughts. "I went to see Richard yesterday because I didn't like the way he had been treating me lately."

"In any particular respect?"

"Off-hand attitudes – changes of plan when we'd arranged to meet – all the classic tell-tales that make you think there's something going wrong with a relationship."

"But I would have thought," began Constable tentatively, "that in a situation such as yours ..."

"What, you mean that the mistress has to put up with what she's given?" interrupted Sarah bitterly.

"Not exactly what I was going to say ..." said the inspector.

"But it wasn't just that," continued Sarah forcefully, the bit now firmly between her teeth. "I'd heard whispers that he was involved with someone else. That's one of the most wonderful things about living in the country, inspector – you've always got friends who are only too pleased to bring you up to date with all the local news. Charming friends that you meet at parties who smile to your face and then cheerfully plunge the knife in when your back is turned. Oh, they never say anything specific, you know. Just those little venomous hints – 'Do you know, I never realised that Richard was friends with so-and-so' and 'Wasn't it kind of Richard to give so-

and-so that private tour of the stables? He's never done that for me'. But that was just Richard. He was always the same. He couldn't help enjoying the company of women. But it's never been serious before."

"And this time?"

"Apparently so."

"Were you aware of who this person was?"

"No. Sadly, the dear friends never passed on that particular piece of information. But I shouldn't be at all surprised if it weren't one of those horse-faced women from the polo club. He'd never been that interested in polo before, but just lately he'd been spending more time going to see the matches at Buldray Park."

"And not in your company?"

"No. Polo has never amused me, inspector. The men may be attractive, but some of the women are vile."

"So you say you went to see Sir Richard yesterday to have it out with him?"

"Yes. I told him I didn't want anything more to do with him, and then I walked out."

"And drove home?"

"No, inspector. I hadn't driven. I'd walked up. There's a footpath just along the lane which leads up through the park to the house. So I walked home, and just as well, because it gave me a chance to cool off."

"Did you see anyone else during your walk? Anyone who might be able to verify your movements?"

"Not a soul, inspector. The back lanes of

Knaggs End aren't exactly lively at that hour."

"And what did you do when you got home?"

Sarah's mouth twisted in a bitter smile. "Had a very large gin and pondered on the meaning of life."

"Were you alone in the house?"

"Yes."

"What I mean is, do you live here alone? What about Mr. Wadsworth?"

"Stuart? My husband," coolly explained Sarah, "lives here at weekends. During the week, he lives in the flat in St. Katherine's Dock in London. He works in the City. In insurance."

"And ... how can I put this ...?"

"Let me save you the trouble, inspector. You want to know how much of all this my husband knew. We have a very understanding marriage. He has his life in London during the week, and I have my life here. At the weekends, we live here together. Very happily."

Constable blinked slightly. "I'm pleased to hear that, Mrs. Wadsworth."

"So let me also save you the trouble of considering whether a jealous husband might have taken it into his head to do away with the 'other man'. The idea is ridiculous. Stuart and I have a perfectly amicable arrangement which some people might find bizarre, but which suits us very well. You may not approve, inspector, but that's the way it is. If you lived in the country, you might not find it quite as shocking as you apparently do."

"It really isn't up to me to make moral judgements, Mrs. Wadsworth, ..."

"And furthermore, inspector," sailed on Sarah, "Stuart could not possibly have been responsible for Richard's death, since he was out dining with a business associate last evening. He telephoned me from the restaurant bar in Chelsea before they went in to eat."

"Are you positive that that was where he was?"

Sarah appeared irritated. "Of course I am. And before you ask, he put his client on the phone for a moment, because it was a Japanese businessman who had met me once at a function and who wanted to pay his respects. So unless you are proposing to advance the theory of some sort of international conspiracy, I really think you are backing the wrong horse."

"And this telephone call came when?" enquired Constable mildly.

"About eight-thirty. Just after I'd got back."

The inspector reflected for a moment. "Yes, well, that all seems to dove-tail very neatly, Mrs. Wadsworth." He got to his feet. "So we'll keep you from your ride no longer. But I dare say if there's anything further we need to ask you, we shall be able to find you."

Sarah looked amused. "Well, I can assure you, Mr. Constable, that I've no intention of fleeing the country, if that was what was in your mind. Happy?"

"Perfectly, Mrs. Wadsworth. Thank you for your time. Come along, sergeant – let's leave the lady to it." With a nod, he led the way back out to the car and, without a further word, reversed out of the drive. After only a few yards, he pulled in to the side of the road, switched off the engine, and took a deep breath.

"Guv, ..." hesitated Dave Copper.

"Sergeant?"

"Can I make a suggestion?"

"Go on."

Copper glanced at his watch. "I reckon a lack of nourishment is beginning to take its toll. And being the time it is, and being as there's a pub on the corner, what say we recharge the batteries with some lunch on the hoof? There's not much wrong that a pint and a ploughman's can't put right. And we've got to stay in the village anyway, because that's where our next interview is. What do you think?"

Constable laughed grudgingly. "You know me too well, sergeant. I've been patronised by experts, but that woman takes the biscuit. And since policemen shall not live by detecting alone, I suppose we ought to go and have some bread to redress the balance. All right, maybe something a bit tastier. Although that pint might have to be reduced to a half, or there could be repercussions. I don't need to face questions about detectives conducting investigations with alcohol on their breath. Let's go and see what this pub has to offer." He restarted the car and let in the clutch.

*

The lounge bar of the Four Horseshoes was characterised by a huge inglenook fireplace filled with an artistic arrangement of logs and conifer branches, a wealth of dark oak beams, and a profusion of leather-mounted horse brasses, many of them, in Andy Constable's estimation, quite possibly genuine. A chalked blackboard listed the menu on offer for the day. Food ordered, the detectives settled themselves with their drinks at a table overlooking the High Street.

"She was a bit much, guv, wasn't she? Mrs. Wadsworth?"

"County type," returned Constable. "Some of them have a habit of regarding the rest of humanity as a rather lesser form of life."

"Isn't this all the sort of thing that Jilly Cooper writes about, sir?" remarked Dave Copper with a grin. "I never expected to find myself in one of her books. Not that I've ever read any of them," he added hastily. "I'm not really much of a one for chick-lit. But as for Mrs. Wadsworth, she's not quite as much of a mystery as we thought. It's all a bit clichéd, if you think about it. Older man in the big house, and posh bird on the side in the village."

"Yes, well, we'll avoid the clichés if we can, sergeant," said Constable. "We probably already have more than enough of those in this case as it is."

"But she certainly did have a motive, didn't she? It wasn't exactly what you'd call a stable relationship. I mean, if she was steamed up about the way Sir Richard was treating her, carrying on with some other woman. Hell hath no fury, and all that. "

"Ah, but according to the way she tells it, she'd already taken care of the problem by deciding to call the whole thing off. So why go that step further and kill him? Unless there's some other factor we don't know about."

"I'll tell you one thing that struck me, though, guv," said Copper. "She seemed quite eager, in a subtle sort of way, to provide an alibi for herself, and for that husband of hers. And without being asked, too. Do we ask ourselves why?"

"Maybe we do, sergeant," agreed Constable. "And there's another thing. You may not have noticed. Everybody else we've spoken to was on the scene of the murder at the time or shortly afterwards, so they know what happened. Well, what we think happened. I'm not jumping to too many conclusions until I hear what SOCO and the doc have to say. But Mrs. Wadsworth wasn't on the scene. And as far as I'm aware, even though there might have been a report of the death on the news, it could only have been sketchy at best. No cause of death would have been mentioned. So I'm wondering how come it didn't occur to the lady to ask how Sir Richard died."

"Good point, sir. But I'll tell you another thing I did pick up on, if I read it right. It looks as if the slightly oily Mr. Worcester was carrying a torch for Mrs. Wadsworth."

"Yes, he was somewhat oleaginous, sergeant, wasn't he?" agreed Constable. "Damp handshake, too. I never trust a man with sweaty palms. Pure prejudice, of course. It means nothing. If you were carrying that much excess weight, you'd sweat. But you're right. If what she seemed to be saying was true, that needn't have stopped him fancying her. Although I much prefer your expression. 'Carrying a torch' sounds a great deal more tasteful."

"So," continued Copper, developing his

thought, "might that have given him some sort of motive to do away with Sir Richard? You know, get his rival out of the way, and then step in and comfort the grieving ..."

"Mistress?" smiled Constable. "It's all a mite tenuous. From the way she was talking, I don't think he would have been in with much of a chance. Plus there's the fact that, as it turns out, he didn't need to take any such drastic action. Mrs. Wadsworth had very neatly removed that particular obstacle in his way by finishing with Sir Richard on that very evening."

"Ah, but Mr. Worcester didn't know that, did he, guv?" countered Copper. "Their paths never crossed. He was there at the house in the afternoon, but he didn't come back until after Sir Richard was dead, by which time it seems as if Mrs. Wadsworth was long gone."

"Hmmm." Constable did not look convinced. "I'm inclined to think that crimes of passion tend to be more of a female province. However, plenty of time to go into these matters later. In the meantime, it looks as if our lunch is heading this way."

The beef cobbler was excellent. As the detectives finished their coffee afterwards, Dave Copper sat gazing out of the window at the High Street.

"There's more to this place than I expected, guv," he remarked. "Most of those villages we passed through were just a few houses, a church, and a little shop if you were lucky. This seems all a bit more substantial. Tea-room, knick-knack shop, 'Dexter Hall's Florists', Supermarket Express – hey, they've even got a betting shop. Look over there – 'Short Odds', it's called."

"Well then," said Constable, "it's evidently a thriving community. And as for the bookie's, I don't think you ought to be surprised. I would have thought that any enterprising bookmaker would seize the chance to cash in on the local interest in the Effingham stables in order to make a bob or two. Anyway, if you can tear your mind away from the prospect of repeating your stroke of good fortune at Goodwell, we'll get back to business and go and see the next one on your list. Which would be ...?"

Copper produced his notebook. "Baverstock ..." he murmured in an undertone, leafing through the pages, "... Worcester ... Wadsworth ... Elliott! Owen Elliott, sir."

"The jockey? The one who rode your ill-fated winner?"

"Yes, guv. And Owen Elliott was the other one who turned up at the house just after the shooting."

"For reasons we have yet to discover. Well, let us go and see him. What's the address?"

"It's 18b, High Street, sir. Looks as if it's a flat ... ha!" Copper guffawed.

"And what is so amusing, sergeant?"

"Just a funny coincidence, sir. It's the flat above the bookie's. There's a thing!"

"I never trust coincidences," remarked Constable drily. "Specially not in a murder case. I like to drag my facts out, kicking and screaming, instead of having them handed to me on a plate. It makes me nervous. Let's go and see if Mr. Elliott is at home, and what he's got to say for himself."

Chapter 7

The young man who answered the rather shabby front door to one side of the entrance to the bookmaker's premises looked haggard. Less than medium height, slim, and in his late twenties, with floppy dark hair and blue eyes with dark circles under them, he regarded the detectives apprehensively.

"Mr. Owen Elliott?"

"Who wants to know?" The voice, low but clear, held a touch of the local burr.

Andy Constable produced his credentials. "I'm Detective Inspector Constable, sir, and this is Detective Sergeant Copper."

"Oh. Right. I thought you might be reporters. I've already had two on the phone this morning."

"On the matter of Sir Richard Effingham? We're making enquiries into his death, sir."

"Yes, Ed told me it was on the news."

"Ed?"

"Yes. Ed Short. It's his betting shop downstairs. He came up and told me what they were saying on the radio this morning."

"But of course you knew all about it, since you were at Sir Richard's house last night, weren't you, sir? And we'd like to ask you some questions about that. So may we come in, please? I'm sure we'll all be more comfortable than standing here on the doorstep."

"Oh. Yes. Come on up." Owen led the way up the stairs into a rather untidy sitting room. "You'd better sit down." He subsided on to an oversized beanbag.

"So, Mr. Elliott, I gather you're a jockey," began Constable, taking a seat on the somewhat shabby sofa as Copper positioned himself behind it, notebook at the ready.

"Huh," grunted Owen. "I would be if I still had a job."

"I was under the impression that you rode for the Effingham stables," said Constable in surprise.

"That's right, guv," broke in Dave Copper. "In fact, I saw Mr. Elliott ride not so long ago – I was at Goodwell to watch the Five Thousand Guineas, sir. You won the race on 'Last Edition', didn't you?"

"Something of a triumph, I gather," commented Constable.

"Yeah, right," replied Owen. "Well, that just goes to show you can never take anything for granted in racing. Up one minute, down the next. And as for 'Last Edition', not my favourite animal at the moment. Brilliant horse, but he's what got me the sack."

"Sir Richard had sacked you?" Constable's attention sharpened. "Would you mind telling us how this came about, sir? And what this had to do with the horse?"

"You know it died?"

"Yes, sir. Some sort of accident, we understand."

"Well, I wish to god the old man had been as understanding as you."

"Perhaps you'd care to explain," said Constable patiently. "We don't know the full circumstances."

"It was supposed to be just an ordinary training session." Owen sat gazing unfocussed into the middle distance, obviously visualising the scene in his mind's eye. "Well, not even that, really. All the other horses had gone up to the gallops, but 'Last Edition' had had a pretty strenuous day at the race meeting the day before, so he got to have a lie-in." He smiled faintly. "I just went up to see him."

"You have a car?"

"Scooter. Never got around to learning to drive a car."

"Go on."

Owen gave a watery smile. "I took him an apple to say thanks for the win. He was a bit perky, so I thought I'd take him out for a breath of fresh air. Just a gentle trot round the *manège* – nothing strenuous. But he took it into his head to go over one of the practice fences. It's a stupid little thing – it's only a couple of feet high, for goodness sake. But he landed awkwardly for some reason. I've got no idea why. He's been over fences two or three times that height hundreds of times. But his left foreleg went from under him. And I heard a crack as he went down, and suddenly I'm picking myself up and looking at him hobbling around on three legs."

"So what did you do then?"

Owen sighed. "Nothing much we could do. When something like that happens to a thoroughbred, you just know it's the end of everything. And there was nobody else about – just me and a couple of the stable lads. So Tina phoned the vet ..."

"Sorry, sir," interrupted Copper. "Tina?"

"One of the lads."

"Tina's a lad?" Copper sounded puzzled.

"They're all lads," explained Owen dully. "Even the girls."

"Do go on, Mr. Elliott," encouraged Constable, with a sideways glance of irritation at his junior. "Tina phoned the vet ...?"

"And she also called Sir Richard. And he said he'd come up, but by the time he arrived, it was all over. The vet had got there first, and he said that the horse was in pain and nothing could be done. And that was it."

"And what was Sir Richard's reaction?"

"What do you think?" replied Owen bitterly. "He was absolutely fuming. He said the whole thing was my fault, and I had no business taking 'Last Edition' out without authority, and he sacked me on the spot. Told me to get out, and if he had his way, I'd never ride again. I tried to explain that it wasn't my fault, and Tina backed me up, but he was in such a rage he wouldn't listen. So here I am, inspector. Unemployed and skint. And probably nobody else will touch me. And now you know everything."

"Not quite everything, sir," contradicted Constable. "We don't know what took you to Sir Richard's house yesterday."

A wary look came into Owen's eyes. "You know I didn't get there until after he died, right? I mean, they did tell you that, didn't they?"

"We do have an approximate list of people's movements," said the inspector. "But that doesn't tell us why you went to the house."

Owen bit his lip. "Desperation, I suppose. I

thought I'd have one last try to persuade him to give me my job back. You know, once the heat of the moment had died down. I wanted to appeal to him. I mean, he's known me since I was a little kid. I was always up around the house and the stables when I was young because I just loved being with the horses, and I suppose he sort of took me under his wing. And he and Lady Olivia never had children, so I guess he just thought it was nice having a youngster about the place." A bitter laugh. "What a joke."

"You're a local, then? Your family comes from the village?"

"Yeah, mum was a local girl. She died a couple of months back."

"I'm sorry to hear that, sir."

"Yes. She'd been ill for a while. We were close." Owen sighed. "Anyway, I thought I'd try reminding Sir Richard about everything, but – well, I never got the chance, did I? I got to the house just before half past eight, and I rang the bell, but it took ages before they answered the door, and then it was Mrs. Carruthers. And she told me about the murder. And then she took me through to the kitchen because she said I looked really shocked and I needed a cup of tea. She wanted to put some brandy in it, but I don't drink, so she put about five sugars in. I thought, what the hell, I'm not having to keep my weight down any more, am I? And so I sat in there with her until the police came."

A thought struck Constable. "Remind me, sergeant. I think Mr. Pelham mentioned that Mr. Elliott had made a telephone call to Effingham Hall earlier in the evening. Am I right?"

Copper riffled back through the pages of his notebook. "That's correct, guv. Around seven, by the look of it. It was just before Mrs. Wadsworth's call."

"Mr. Elliott?" Constable looked enquiringly at the jockey.

"Oh. It was just to check that Sir Richard was home."

"And did you actually speak to him?"

"Yes, but only briefly."

"And can you tell us what was said?"

"I just told him I needed to talk to him. And he said not to bother, but I decided to go up anyway."

"On your scooter?"

"Walked."

"I see. And did you see anyone else as you went?"

Owen frowned. "No. I don't think so. Why?"

"Oh, I just wondered if there might be someone who could verify your movements, Mr. Elliott. We always like to double-check our facts if we can. So, then, to sum up, you in fact didn't actually see Sir Richard yesterday at all? And although you were in his bad books, so to speak, after the incident with 'Last Edition', you still cherished hopes that you might be able to persuade him to rescind his decision?"

"That's about it."

Constable rose to his feet. "Then that probably is about it for the time being, sir." He paused. "Oh, just one thing. I assume that, until recently at least, you would have been quite close to

Sir Richard. I'm wondering if you can think of anyone in his circle who might have had any reason to wish him ill."

Owen shook his head. "Racing's not really like that, inspector. Okay, there's a lot of rivalry, but it's all pretty friendly. Civilised, I suppose you could say. I mean, most of the jockeys could be riding for one owner one day and then somebody else the next."

"And the owners and trainers? How about the financial side of things?"

Owen gave a wan smile. "I don't think anyone involved with racing does it to get rich, inspector. The only ones who manage to do that are the bookies. You want to ask Ed Short about that."

"Perhaps we'll do just that, sir."

*

As they stood once again on the pavement outside Owen Elliott's front door, Dave Copper was intrigued by the speculative look in Andy Constable's eyes. "Something on your mind, guv?"

"I'm just thinking," replied the inspector. "Maybe Mr. Elliott's suggestion wasn't such a stupid one. It occurs to me that somebody like a bookmaker needs to have the inside track on what's going on in the world where he makes his money. If he hasn't got all the right information at his fingertips, he could easily catch a cold by offering silly odds on dead certs, or what have you." He laughed. "I haven't a clue what I'm talking about, really. All this world of betting is a completely closed book to me. But I've got an instinct that somebody like this Mr. Short might have a knowledge of the sort of gossip which could fill in a few gaps in the formal statements. It's worth checking out."

"You, going into a betting shop in the middle of an investigation, guv?" grinned Copper. "You'd better hope that never gets out. Well, after you." He pushed open the shop door and held the plastic slashed curtain aside to allow his superior to enter.

The establishment was devoid of customers. Above a shelf littered with pens, odd pieces of paper, and untidily discarded daily newspapers, a bank of television screens, volumes reduced to a murmur, provided mumbled commentaries on various sporting events. A large and complex-looking electronic gaming machine, tones warbling in an endless barrage of sound, flashed a persistent and repetitious invitation to play its game in the hope of winning enticing amounts of cash. And behind a grille, a young woman looked up from her task of filing a scarlet talon, manoeuvred her chewing gum to the side of her mouth, and directed a well-practised mechanical smile towards her visitors. "Afternoon, gents. Come to put a last-minute bet on today's big event?"

"Not exactly," said Constable. "We were wondering if it would be possible to have a word with Mr. Short."

"He's not available," came the automatic reply. "Who wants him?"

Constable produced his warrant card. "My colleague and I are from the county police. And we hoped that Mr. Short might be free for an informal chat."

"Oh." The woman was clearly thrown off balance. "Um. Let me see if I can find him." She eased herself off her stool and picked up a wall phone at the rear of her booth. "Hello, Ed," she muttered into it, obviously attempting to keep her voice as low as possible. "There's a couple of blokes out here from the police. They want you. What shall I tell them? ... Oh. Okay." She hung up the phone and turned back with a further attempt at a carefree smile. "That's lucky. He was in the office after all. He'll be out in just a sec."

A door at the rear of the shop opened, and a figure emerged. "Officers of the law come to see me? Well, that's a pleasant surprise. Come into the office, gents, and we'll see what we can do to help." A gesture invited the detectives to enter his sanctum.

Ed Short was as far from the conventional image of a traditional bookmaker as it was possible to be. No loudly-chequered suit straining across a squat chubby frame, no cheery rubicund face, no fairground barker's accent, no fat cigar jammed into the corner of the mouth. Tall, something over six feet, and cadaverously thin, his pasty complexion and dark charcoal grey suit made him look more like an undertaker than anything else. The voice was unschooled, with a carefully-applied veneer of cultivation. "So, what have I done to attract the attentions of the police?" he enquired, with a toothy smile which did not quite reach his eyes, as he settled back into the large and capacious leather chair behind his desk.

"Nothing at all, sir, as far as I'm aware," responded the inspector comfortably. He took a seat opposite the bookmaker on one of the bentwood chairs which seemed to have been designed specifically to make any visitor feel ill-at-ease. "Let me introduce myself and my colleague." He did so with the accompanying presentation of warrant cards. "We are looking into the death of Sir Richard Effingham, and we hoped you might be able to assist us with some additional information."

"But I don't know anything about it, other than what they said on the news," protested Ed.

"I'm sure that's true, sir," said Constable. "No, it's more the facts around the periphery of the case where we thought you might be able to contribute."

"How do you mean?"

"I find myself slightly surprised that your shop is here at all, Mr. Short." Constable declined to tackle the subject directly. "I freely admit I know very little about the world you inhabit, but I should have thought that in these days of online betting, a business like this in a country area would be struggling against the odds for survival."

"Oh, very amusing, Mr. Constable," said Ed. A thin smile. "We do enjoy a good pun around here. Hence the name of the shop. Just my tiny joke. And some of my customers like to call me Short Ed. What with the horse-racing, you see."

'The long winter evenings must just whiz by,' mused Constable, but he wisely kept the thought to himself.

"But as regards the business," went on Ed, "in fact, you couldn't be more wrong. We've got quite a lively clientèle here. I'm the only turf accountant for miles around, and people do like to come in for a chat and to swap a few tips. We get pretty busy, specially on big race days. People tend to like to watch in a crowd, even if they lose."

"Misery loves company, I suppose," murmured Constable in an undertone. "And there would be the additional local interest, I imagine," he went on aloud. "With the village being the home of a prominent trainer."

"That's true, inspector. It certainly doesn't do any harm. And of course, I was a great fan of Sir Richard's anyway."

"Sir?"

"His books, inspector. If there's one thing I enjoy, it's a good murder mystery, and I loved the ones Sir Richard wrote. I didn't actually know he was the author when I first discovered them, because he wrote under another name, and you could have knocked me down with a feather when I found out. In a way, he was good for business – you know, raising the general level of interest in horse-racing meant that more people were inclined to have a flutter now and again, so me buying his books was just returning the favour, in a way. And now, poor man, he's in a murder mystery of his own. I suppose it is a mystery, inspector? I mean, you don't know who did it?"

"Not as yet, Mr. Short," said Constable. "Which is why we're interested in gleaning any additional facts from wherever we can."

"I don't see how I can help," said Ed, shrugging. "I had next to no dealings with Sir Richard personally."

"Ah, but your tenant upstairs is a very different matter, sir. We gather that Mr. Elliott and Sir Richard had a great deal to do with one another."

101

Ed shook his head sadly. "Owen? Yes, he's a talented boy. He's made quite a lot of money over the years."

"I wasn't aware that jockeys were particularly well-paid."

"No, I meant that he'd made money for the owners and trainers. Prize money and the like. And of course, if a stallion is successful, there's no limit to what it can make in stud fees."

"But surely some of this must have come Mr. Elliott's way. And of course, knowing the horses he was riding, he must have been able to clock up some appreciable winnings from people like yourself."

"Oh no, inspector. You're quite wrong. Jockeys aren't allowed to bet. Or trainers, for that matter. Not that some of them don't, and I could name one or two where they've caught a pretty big cold as a result." Ed cleared his throat, realising he was teetering on the edge of an indiscretion. "Naming no names, of course. No, the rules are very strict. Mind you ..." A crafty look came over the bookmaker's face. "... there's nothing to stop jockeys passing a few words of advice on to their friends. Purely unofficially, of course. Helps to set the odds, if nothing else. Well, there's no chance of that with Owen in future. It's a shame. He's won a lot of races for Sir Richard, and I think it's very unfortunate that it's ended as it has."

"You knew Mr. Elliott had lost his job, then?"

"Oh yes, inspector. You can't keep secrets in a place like this."

"I hoped that might be the case, Mr. Short," smiled Constable. "And therefore, you may be able to tell me - strictly confidentially, of course," he added quickly, as Ed seemed about to interrupt, "whether, unlike yourself, there might be anyone else in the vicinity to whom we might usefully speak."

"I hope you aren't inviting me to indulge in vulgar gossip, Mr. Constable."

"Nothing was further from my mind," the inspector reassured him. "I'm thinking more in terms of local colour."

"Well ..." Ed hesitated. "You could have a word with Sarah Wadsworth. She knew Sir Richard quite well, by all accounts."

"We have, in fact, spoken to Mrs. Wadsworth, sir. I think we're fairly clear on the situation there."

"Oh." There was obvious disappointment in Ed's tone. "Well, in that case, I suppose it wouldn't do any harm to talk to Susan."

'Another one?' thought Constable. "And this would be Susan ...?" he enquired.

"Susan Robson-Bilkes. She's the local solicitor," explained Ed. "Her office is just across the road. I don't know for sure, but she's probably got her finger on the pulse of most of what goes on around here. Mind you, after the row about the book, she and Sir Richard might not have been on the best of terms."

"Row about the book?" echoed Constable, intrigued. "Tell me more."

"You don't know? Well, I am surprised. It was quite the talking point around here. But as nothing ever came of it, I suppose it never got much further than the village."

"Exactly what are we talking about?" pursued the inspector.

Ed leaned back, seemingly prepared to enjoy himself. "It was his big best-seller – 'Murder For The Defence'. You know it?"

"I've heard of it."

"Well, in that, there's a lawyer who, it turns out, is up to her neck in corruption. Crime families, and so on. All sorts of fiddles she's got going on, and there's an investigation under way, and somebody gets killed, and in the end they find out that she's the one who did it."

'Thanks for the spoiler alert,' thought Constable. "But I don't see ..."

"And the thing was, Susan got it into her head that Sir Richard had based the character on her. You know, age and appearance and what-have-you. Mind you, she wasn't the only one who thought it. You know what they say, write what you know, and her firm had been handling Sir Richard's family affairs for years, and there were so many things in the book which looked as if they were referring to her. So she got hopping mad, even though Sir Richard denied it and put out all sorts of disclaimers and said it was all coincidence, but there was talk of her suing him for libel and everything."

Constable's eyebrows rose. "It sounds as if things got rather lively. So then what happened?"

"Well ... nothing really." Ed seemed conscious of the anticlimax. "It all got smoothed over somehow, by all accounts. I don't exactly know how, and maybe not quite in the way she might have wished, knowing what some people have said about

Sir Richard's liking for the ladies, but that could well have been just tittle-tattle. But there was certainly a bit of talk about the nice new car she got soon afterwards, and she did end up with the leg of one of the horses Sir Richard had in training."

"A leg of ...? Sorry, Mr. Short, I'm not with you." Constable directed a baffled glance at Copper.

"I think he means a stake in the ownership of the horse, sir," explained the sergeant. "It entitles you to a share of its winnings. Sounds to me as if it would have been some sort of peace offering. As opposed to a horse's head in the foot of the bed, guv, which means something quite different."

"I have a feeling we're rather straying from the point, gentlemen," said Constable, a touch of exasperation plain in his voice. "But I'm interested in one thing you say, Mr. Short, which is the fact that this Mrs. Robson-Bilkes ..."

"Miss."

" ... this Miss Robson-Bilkes may well have some knowledge of the Effingham family's affairs. I think that may well be where we next go seeking information."

Chapter 8

The visit to the offices of the law firm of Cheetham and Partners, located in a Georgian town house on the opposite side of the High Street, was fruitless. The door remained firmly shut, the bell remained unanswered. A brass plate announced that clients would only be seen by arrangement. A telephone number was helpfully provided.

"Part-timers, obviously, guv," remarked Dave Copper. "How nice it must be to live in the country, where nothing much goes on except by appointment."

"Unless it happens to be murder, of course," returned Andy Constable drily. "Which tends to throw something of a spanner in the works. Well, take a note of the phone number, and we'll try to track down the lady later. In the meantime, I think it's a case of completing the circuit and returning to Effingham Hall."

As the car came to a halt at the foot of the front door steps, the detectives could see a figure engaged in trimming a group of shrubs to the right, adjacent to the corner of the house. Tweed cap pushed to the back of his head, sleeves on the collarless grey shirt rolled to the elbows, and brown corduroy trousers above a pair of sturdy scuffed boots, it was not hard to deduce that here was the gardener who had assisted the unfortunate Inspector Fletcher in his encounter with Lady Effingham's horse. The figure, who it was plain might well never see eighty again, straightened with a slight groan as Constable approached.

106

"Good afternoon." Constable delved into his memory. "It's Mr. Diggory, isn't it?"

"That's right, sir." Milky blue eyes regarded the detectives out of a seamed weather-beaten face. The accent was a ringing testimony to the gardener's local roots. "And you'll be the police gentlemen that Mr. Pelham said were going round asking questions."

"We are indeed, sir. I'm Inspector Constable – this is Sergeant Copper – and if we're not tearing you away from your work, we'd like a word."

"I don't know as I can tell you much, being as I wasn't here last night," said Diggory, laying aside his hedge clippers and seeming more than ready to take advantage of a distraction from his duties. "I was away up at home. But you're welcome to ask away, anything you want. In fact, I'm more or less done here, so if you can hold on a minute, I'll just finish clearing up, and then we can go round to my little snug and I can rest my old bones over a cup of tea." He gathered up the sheet of clippings from beneath the bush he had been trimming and bundled it into his wheelbarrow, together with his shears. "It's this way, gents." He rounded the corner of the house and plunged into a thick shrubbery, dense with rhododendrons and all manner of evergreens, following a gravel path which snaked through the undergrowth. A branch of the path led off to the right and seemed to continue in the direction of the park.

"That must be the path that leads down to the village, guv," pointed out Copper. "The one that Mrs. Wadsworth was talking about."

107

"That's right, sir," agreed Diggory over his shoulder. "Comes out the other side of here, down through the fern garden, and then straight across the park. Cuts off the big loop of the drive, so it's much quicker if you just want to get down to the village. I always go down that way on my bike. 'Course, it's not so easy coming back up at my age." He gave a slightly wheezy cackle.

"Is that the only route?"

"That's right."

"Hold on, guv." Copper stopped abruptly. He lowered his voice. "If that's the only way to the village, we've got some contradictions. You remember Sarah Wadsworth told us she didn't see anyone else on her way to and from the village, and Owen Elliott said much the same thing. But with the timings we've got, they should by rights have been in the same place at the same time. They should have come face to face with one another. So it looks as if one of them isn't telling us the truth. The question is, which one?"

"You may be on to something, sergeant," agreed Constable in similarly lowered tones. "So, Mr. Diggory," he said aloud, "you're telling us that anyone using this path would be bound to see another person taking the same route?"

"Ah," said Diggory. "No, I didn't say that."

"Then ... then I'm confused, Mr. Diggory. What exactly are you saying?"

The gardener put down the wheelbarrow handles. "It's easy, inspector. Look for yourself. This old shrubbery's a bit of a maze. You can see, there's that path there we've just come past, but there's another one just round the corner here that we're just about to come to. And then, when you get down to the fernery, there's the direct path round the edge, or there's the little winding one that wriggles through, or there's the steps that go down through the grotto." He chuckled. "That one was always a favourite with the kids. I remember when Master James was young, he always used to hide in there and then pop out to try to make people jump. Bit of a rascal, he always was."

"So, in fact, there is no reason why two people coming and going at the same time would necessarily be aware of one another?"

"No, none at all. Course, you've also got the little drive which goes round outside the fernery to the stable yard, for taking the cars round to the back. Used to be for the carriages in the old days, of course. Why, is it important?"

"No, not in the slightest, Mr. Diggory," replied Constable airily. And in an aside to Copper, "Another theory crashes to the ground."

Diggory opened a door, half concealed by foliage, in the tall brick wall which butted up to the side of the house, and pushed his barrow through into the cobbled yard which lay beyond, empty save for a graphite-grey sports car of the type which was virtually part of the uniform for smart young men in the City. Diggory held open a door which led into an outbuilding, dimly-lit through cobwebbed windows, where racks of gardening tools hung on the walls alongside dusty shelves which housed a miscellany of rusty tins with scrawled labels, battered cardboard boxes, and anonymous paper packets.

"Here's my little cubby-hole. Sit yourselves down, gents," he said, indicating an ancient-looking wooden settle against one wall. "Now, I'm going to have meself a cup of tea. Thirsty work, gardening." He switched on a battered electric kettle and plopped a tea bag into an enamel mug which had clearly seen better days, adding milk and sugar at the same time. "I could do you one if you like. I got some more mugs here somewhere."

The detectives exchanged dubious looks. "It's very kind of you, Mr. Diggory," said Constable. "But we wouldn't want to put you to any trouble."

"Ah well, suit yourselves," said Diggory, pouring the boiling water on to the brew and stirring with a shaky hand. He hung his cap on a hook, lowered himself into an elderly fireside chair under the window, and looked expectantly at the detectives. "So, gents, what is it you want to know?"

"I suppose we'd better start with your full name, sir," said Constable. "And I hope you won't mind if Sergeant Copper here makes some notes."

"You go right ahead, boy," said Diggory. "I ain't got nothing to hide. And as for the name, it's Elias Jeroboam Diggory. Want me to spell that for you?"

"I don't think that'll be necessary, sir," replied Copper, concealing a smile. "I think I can manage that, even though I don't run across too many Elias Jeroboams in the average day."

"Proper god-fearing woman, my mother," said Diggory. "My old dad wanted me called Joe after him, but he didn't get a look-in. Not with none of us. Youngest of six, I was. All gone now, of course."

"And you've worked here for some time?"

"Oh, donkey's years. Practically all my life. My old dad was a gardener here too before the war, so really it's a bit of a family business. 'Course, then there was a whole bunch of staff here, but now there's just me out here in the gardens. I keep 'em up as best I can, and Sir Richard and her ladyship have always seemed happy enough. I mean, the wages ain't so much, but Sir Richard lets me live in the little North Lodge down the back drive, so I've never had to pay a penny rent. He was good like that."

Constable resumed the questioning. "What we're after, Mr. Diggory, is whatever additional information we can gather about the events of yesterday."

"Ah, well, like I said, I wasn't there when they had all the trouble, so I don't really know what you want me to tell you. You see I don't really come into the house very often – just into the kitchen sometimes, when Mrs. Carruthers does me a cup of tea or a bit of snap, and then she always makes sure I take my boots off. She's a very particular woman, is our Mrs. Carruthers. Nice, though."

"I was thinking more about what happened earlier on in the day. Perhaps you can help us with that. Were you out and about in the grounds at all?"

"Most of the day."

"And there were some comings and goings at various times, I think?" coaxed Constable.

"Oh, plenty of them," agreed Diggory, taking a long slurp of tea.

"Could you perhaps talk us through them?"

"Well, as best I can. See, I wasn't here all the time, 'cos a couple of mornings a week I don't get up here first thing because I'm working on my vegetable patch at my lodge. I got some beautiful carrots coming on. That's one of the best things about her ladyship keeping Punter here in the old stables, you know – plenty of fertiliser for my garden. Mind you, having said that, I was down here pretty early on, but that was only to get a barrow-load of muck off the heap, and then I had to trundle it all the way back home, which don't seem so bad if you're driving, but that last bit up to the lodge is steeper than it looks. So anyway, I did that, and then I forked it into the spare patch where I'm doing my next bit of planting ..."

"But you did eventually come to the vicinity of the Hall itself?" interrupted Constable, eager to move the gardener on from his horticultural ramblings.

"Ah, well, hold your horses. I was just coming to that," said Diggory placidly, declining to be hurried. "I was coming back to the Hall with my barrow when I sees Master James go past in his car."

"Any idea what time that would have been?" enquired Copper.

"Oh, must have been about eleven o'clock, I suppose," replied the gardener.

"And that was up the drive towards your North Lodge? Not the front drive?"

"That's right. He usually keeps his car in the stable yard round here at the back of the house, see. It's that one out there now. And wherever he parks it, it's always in the way. No consideration. Flashy

112

thing, it is, with its tinted windows and all, but then, they say that's the way it is with these so-called smart city boys. If you ain't got the right car, you get looked down on."

"It sounds, Mr. Diggory," resumed Constable with a slight smile, "that you don't altogether approve of Mr. Booker-Gresham."

"Ah, well, not for me to pass judgement on members of the family," said Diggory, perhaps conscious of a slight indiscretion. He stretched his neck to peer out of the window, as if to ensure that he could not be overheard. "But if you want the honest truth, I ain't got a lot of time for him. I mean, he was all right as a boy, but they don't always grow up the way you'd want, do they?" He smiled fondly. "Now that young Mr. Elliott – he's different."

"Owen Elliott? Really?"

"Oh, yes. Chalk and cheese. You couldn't meet a nicer lad. He's exactly the same as when he was a boy in the village."

"You knew him when he was young?"

"'Course. He was always up around the stables when he was a kid. He always had this thing about horses – he just seemed to get on with them. You know, had the knack. And Sir Richard never seemed to mind. In fact, he encouraged him, and I suppose it was only natural that it led on to him becoming a jockey. He had him apprenticed and all. And even these days, it's nothing unusual for him to pop up here to see us, just to say hello and bring Punter an apple or something. Well, I say 'is'. I mean 'was' really, 'cos we ain't seen a lot of him since all the trouble. I s'pose you know all about that – you

113

know, with 'Last Edition' and everything?"

"We have heard the story," said Constable.

"All very sad, that," said Diggory with a sorrowful shake of the head. "But it made him a bit of a ... what is it they say ... *Persona non grata*? ... with Sir Richard."

"That's what we gather," said Constable, slightly surprised by the gardener's venture into Latin legalese. "Which brings us to Sir Richard himself. Did you see him at all during the day?"

"Oh, that wouldn't have been until later. Afternoon, it was ... just after lunchtime, I reckon." He screwed up his eyes in recollection. "Yes, that'd be about right. I was getting some weed out of the lily pond in the west garden, and Sir Richard came round from the front of the house with Mrs. Baverstock, and they were having a right old to-do. They didn't notice me because they were up above me on the west terrace, see, and I kept my head down, but I could hear what they were saying plain as plain."

"And what was the exact nature of this 'to-do', Mr. Diggory?" asked Constable.

"Well, as it happens, it was all about 'Last Edition'. She was the owner, see, and she must have had great hopes for it, specially after it won the big race. Everybody was going on about it down the pub in the village afterwards, and saying as how that horse must be worth a mint now. In fact, I don't mind admitting, it did me a bit of good, 'cos I had a couple of quid on it myself, thank you very much. All over the papers, it was, and then before you could turn round, it was all over the papers again after it died."

"And this was what she and Sir Richard were talking about?"

"Shouting, more like. And she was laying all the blame on him. Poor old Sir Richard could hardly get a word in edgeways, and that wasn't like him at all. But she said it was all his fault because he should have been keeping proper control over everything that went on up at the training stables, and she wasn't at all sure that there hadn't been something dodgy going on. She said that the horse was worth millions, specially after the Five Thousand Guineas win, and why hadn't the insurance been kept up to date on it, and that she'd make sure he paid."

"What was Sir Richard's reaction to all this?"

"Well, he tried to calm her down as best he could. In fact, he said, why didn't they leave it for now, because they obviously weren't getting anywhere, and he'd want to check up on a few things, so why didn't she come back later in the evening so as to talk it all through over dinner?"

"And she agreed? Well, she must have done so, because we know that she did indeed come back in the evening."

"Ah, well, you'd know that better than me. All I know is, she went off after that, and I caught a glimpse of her face when she was leaving, and she looked to me as if she was still in a right rage."

"And Sir Richard?"

"He just watched her go, and then he went off down the park with Sheba. And I think that's it ... I don't think I saw him at all after that."

Constable paused for a moment to digest the

115

new information. "You said there were plenty of comings and goings during the day, Mr. Diggory. Can you remember anything in particular that struck you about any of those?"

Diggory scratched his head. "Oh, now you're asking. I mean, what do you call partic'lar? Thinking about it, I remember hearing another car out the front at some time, but I was round the side so I never saw it, just heard it, so I couldn't tell you anything about that. I don't have time to go checking up on who comes and goes – I've got my work to do."

"Members of the family?" hazarded the inspector.

"I saw Master James's car again, going round from the front to the stable yard sometime," said the gardener. "Must have been later on, but I couldn't say exactly when."

At Constable's side, Copper gave a small sigh of frustration. "You can't be more precise than that, sir? We always like to be as exact as we can."

Diggory shook his head. "Sorry, sergeant. I can't go looking at my watch every five seconds in case something happens." He suddenly snapped his fingers. "Here, hold on. Maybe you'll like this a bit better. There was another car, but that wasn't till the evening, and I know exactly when that was, on account of the television."

"How come, sir?"

"'Cos it was during the adverts. I'd put on that 'Midwinter Murders' programme – I like a good murder mystery on the telly, me." He paused and pulled a face. "Although I have to say, it feels a bit

116

funny being in the middle of one in real life. Anyway, it was just getting going, and then the first lot of adverts came on, and I always turn the sound off during them 'cos they drive me mad, what with silly girls dancing about trying to sell me sofas and suchlike. So that would have been quarter past eight, near enough on the dot. And that was when I heard a car go past my lodge. I didn't see it, so I don't know whose it was, and I don't know which way it was going. I didn't really think anything of it, and if the sound hadn't been off I doubt if I'd have heard it at all. And then I went and cooked my bit of supper and then I settled down to watch the rest of the programme. Tell the truth, I dozed off for a bit, so I never found out who did it in the end. And then I went to bed, and that's all I know till the police came knocking this morning."

"Could it have been Mr. Booker-Gresham's car?" asked Copper. "You mentioned he keeps it in the yard here."

"I s'pose it must have been. It couldn't have been her ladyship, 'cos she doesn't drive."

"And on the subject of the family, Mr. Diggory," intervened Constable, "you haven't mentioned whether you saw Lady Effingham at all during the day."

"Now as it happens, I did," said Diggory. "That was a bit earlier, when I was still up here at the house, and I can tell you exactly when that was and all."

"Go on, sir," said Copper, encouraged.

"And that was because I did look at my watch," continued the gardener. "See, I'd just

117

finished up, which was just on seven o'clock ..."

"Isn't that rather late to be still working, sir?"

"Ah, well, I hadn't started till late, like I told you, what with doing the work on my own veg patch, so I carried on a bit later, on account of I don't like to take advantage, the family being good to me and all. Anyway, I was just collecting my things up to put away, and that door over there ..." The detectives craned to look as he indicated a door in the wall at the far corner of the stable yard, just beyond the edge of the house. "That door gives on to the north terrace, and I noticed I must have left it open, so I went to close it, and I saw her ladyship down in one of the borders outside the library windows. Lovely little borders, they are – alpines, mostly, which are a particular favourite of her ladyship's, which is why she got me to put them in there in the first place."

"You say she was down in the border?" queried Copper.

"That's right," confirmed Diggory. "Crouched down, she was. I think she must have been pulling up a couple of weeds. Very hot on that, she is – she loves her garden, and she's always telling me if I've missed something. Which I admit I do once in a while, 'cos my eyesight ain't as good as it used to be. Anyway, I ducked back, 'cos to be frank, I didn't want her giving me an earful when I wanted to get off, and when I looked again a couple of minutes later, she'd gone. I thought, dodged a bullet on that one, my lad." The wheezing chuckle returned.

"You saying that reminds me of something I wanted to ask you, Mr. Diggory," resumed Constable. "During last night's events, there was a shot heard.

118

We have information that the weapon involved may have been a shotgun. So tell me, Mr. Diggory ... do you keep a shotgun?"

The gardener gave a pitying look. "'Course I do! Wouldn't be much use trying to look after the gardens at a house like this and not have a shotgun."

"Really, sir?"

"Rabbits," explained Diggory shortly. "They cause havoc, the little perishers. Can't keep them out of some of the flowerbeds, and as for my veg patch, I've had to put all sorts of fencing and netting in, and the little blighters still get through. I have to say, I miss a lot more that I get, but I don't half give them a scare. And then there's pigeons. Nothing better for the pot at the right time of year than a nice plump pigeon. And Mrs. Carruthers, she makes a lovely pigeon pie."

"And you keep this shotgun where?" asked Constable, declining to be sidetracked by culinary considerations. "Safely locked away, I assume?"

"Ah." Diggory shifted evasively. "Well, of course, I've got a cabinet for it. Just in that cupboard there. But I have to admit, I don't always remember to lock it. No need, you see. Not round here."

"May we see?"

"'Course you can. And you'll find it's nice and clean. I always gives it a good clean before I puts it away." The gardener heaved himself to his feet and opened the door of the rather worm-eaten cupboard in the corner. Bolted to the wall within the cupboard was a sturdy metal cabinet. The padlock hung loose. The door stood ajar. The cabinet was empty.

Chapter 9

Leaving behind them a considerably chastened gardener, the detectives made their way back round the house through the shrubbery to where they had left their car on the front drive.

"You're not happy, guv, are you?" remarked Dave Copper. "I can tell."

"What do you think?" retorted Andy Constable. "A firearm left sloshing about, in contravention of all the regulations, and lo and behold, what do we have but a murder where there's a shotgun involved, and no sign of it. Somebody had better find it pretty soon, or else."

"What next then, guv?" enquired Copper. "I can't imagine SOCO aren't already on the case."

Constable consulted his watch. "It's probably too late to do much else today. I rather fancy checking with the SOCO team anyway to see what results they've got for us, but I wouldn't mind betting that they've probably vanished for the day." A quick word with the solitary uniformed officer who stood post outside the front door of Effingham Hall confirmed his surmise. "Right. Decision time. We'll start afresh in the morning. You can make a list. There's that solicitor woman to speak to, if she's deigned to turn up at her office, and if the doctor and SOCO haven't got something worthwhile to tell us by then, I shall want to know the reason why. So, back to home ground, I think. As someone once said, tomorrow is another day."

*

"There's one advantage to working off the

home patch," remarked Andy Constable the following morning, as he pulled past a dawdling caravan and accelerated along a stretch of dual carriageway. "We do get to experience the delights of the English countryside instead of traipsing about our normal urban environment."

"You have to admit, guv," said Dave Copper, "that working off our home patch has turned into something of a habit. I mean, even that holiday in Spain got hijacked by the bloke in the trench. I don't think I'll ever look at a Spanish holiday brochure in quite the same way again."

"Don't be churlish, sergeant," smiled Constable. "You did get a free cruise home out of it. In some considerable luxury, if I recall."

"That's all very well," countered Copper. "But if it's all the same to you, I prefer my nautical dead bodies to turn up in pirate movies rather than on cruise ships."

"Then you'll be all the more pleased that we have a nice normal land-based dead body to deal with on this occasion."

"Not entirely sure that I'd call Sir Richard Effingham a nice normal dead body, sir, according to what Dr. Livermore said on the phone this morning, sir."

"Yes, what exactly did he say?"

"Not actually that much, guv. He seemed a bit reluctant to go into too much detail, and I think he was in a bit of a rush because he said he had an exhumation to go to. Apparently somebody's been accused of leaving bits of medical ironmongery inside people during operations at the local hospital, and they were digging up one of the supposed victims."

"Charming! Couldn't they just go along with a metal detector, instead of hauling some poor soul out of their grave?"

"Now that, guv, if I may say so, sounds like the sort of off-colour remark which you're always ticking me off for."

"You're right, sergeant," agreed Constable with a smile. "You're obviously proving a bad influence on me. So, how long is this proposed excavation going to take, do we know?"

"Only a couple of hours, guv. But it's no problem, because I also spoke to Sergeant Singleton on the SOCO team, and they're expecting us any time this morning, so we can fit them in first, before we go on to the mortuary."

"This is all very organised. Well done. And how about our elusive lady solicitor?"

"Susan Robson-Bilkes? Still being elusive, I'm afraid, sir. I've tried a couple of times, but it goes straight to voice-mail. I'll keep trying."

"Do. If there's anything in what Ed Short told us and she had some sort of animus against Sir Richard, we want to know the nuts and bolts of it to see whether we need to add her name to our list of persons of interest. Now, let me concentrate," said Constable, as the car began to enter the straggling outskirts of Westchester. "I haven't been this way for quite a while, but if my memory serves me correctly, the main police station should be somewhere along here on the right."

"Used to be, sir," corrected Copper. "They

moved out last year. Apparently they've got a shiny new H.Q. Just near the railway station. Sergeant Singleton says if you just follow the British Rail symbol on the road signs, it'll take you straight there."

The town's new police premises were indeed striking. Seven ultra-modern storeys of mirrored glass interspersed with panels of shining steel and vivid red cladding, topped with an impressive array of aerials, gave a clear statement that the forces of law and order were present in strength, and meant undoubted business. After a brief word and a flash of credentials at the barrier, Constable pulled into the car park and, Copper in tow, climbed the flight of steps to the front door, which was, he noted, flanked by a pair of incongruously-traditional blue lamps. Directed by the reception desk, the two detectives took the lift to the sixth floor. As the lift door opened, Sergeant Una Singleton stood waiting to welcome them.

"Good morning, sir. Sergeant." She greeted the detectives with a smile for Constable and an even warmer one for Copper. "Front Desk told us you were on your way up, so I thought I'd give you the personal conducted tour. If you'd like to come this way." She led the way along a brightly-lit corridor between a series of open-plan offices whose windows gave views over the roofs of the town below, and through a double swing door into a large laboratory dazzling with the gleam of spotlights, stainless steel, and brilliant white work surfaces. Operatives, singly or in murmuring pairs, were dotted about at benches or workstations, intent on their observations and analyses of the items before them. Floor-to-ceiling windows along one wall gave an uninterrupted vista over the suburbs below, which rapidly petered out into a patchwork of greenery as the countryside beyond faded towards a hazy horizon.

Constable paused in admiration. "I can see why you put in for that transfer, sergeant," he remarked. "This is all extremely glamorous and state-of-the-art. It's a far cry from the gloomy burrow our team has to work in back at base."

"It is that, sir," agreed Singleton.

"Don't you get distracted by the views?" asked Copper, as a wheeling flock of starlings swept past the window. "I know I would."

"We try not to," smiled the SOCO officer. "And sometimes, if the sunsets are just too beautiful, we force ourselves to close the blinds."

"My heart bleeds," muttered Copper.

"And delightful though it be," continued the inspector, "we haven't actually come here to admire the view. I'm hoping for a rather more close-up look at things."

"I think we can manage that, sir," said Singleton. "In fact, I've laid all the relevant material out on the table in the conference room next door."

"Then let's take a look at it."

"Would you like a coffee before we start, sir?"

"Always sharpens my brain cells, guv," put in Copper with a hopeful expression.

"Well, in that case," said Constable, "on the remote off-chance that Copper's brain cells will be needed, I suppose I'd better say yes."

"Jason," Singleton called across to one of her young colleagues, who looked barely old enough to be dissecting frogs in a secondary school classroom. "Can you rustle up a pot of coffee and three mugs for us. Thanks." She opened a door and ushered the two detectives into a room adjoining the lab, where a range of items, all encased in protective plastic coverings, were spread out along the top of a large table. "And here we have it."

"And what precisely is 'it'?" enquired Constable. "Although I don't need to ask in respect of that particular one. I remember that very well indeed."

"The dagger?" replied Singleton, picking it up and handing it to the inspector for closer examination. "I imagine the last time you saw it, it was still in the victim's chest."

"Buried up to the hilt, if I remember correctly," said the inspector, with a slight inward shudder.

"And exceptionally sharp," warned Singleton, "so you should be careful how you handle it."

"And let me guess – you're saying that it is so sharp that it wouldn't take a great deal of force to drive it home?"

"That's right."

"And therefore no help in deciding the sort of person who might have used it."

"Probably not, sir," admitted Singleton.

Constable sighed. "Does it tell us anything? Prints?" He did not sound particularly hopeful.

The SOCO officer shook her head. "Sadly not, sir. Some smudges where they might have been, but they're not even clear enough to be positive about that. Certainly nothing we can lift a DNA sample off. Somebody has made what I might describe as an amateurish but annoyingly effective attempt at wiping the thing clean."

"Any information regarding exactly what it is?"

"Oh, that's the easiest part, sir. Two minutes on the internet tells you pretty much everything you need to know. It's a genuine antique, most probably Turkish, seventeenth century. There's one remarkably like it in the Topkapi Palace museum in Istanbul. Damascened steel blade, silver handle studded with genuine precious stones, including that particularly impressive cabochon emerald, with a couple of pieces of rather nice filigree work."

"And sounding very valuable."

"More than likely, sir. We haven't got around to assessing value. It seemed the last thing to be thinking about."

"Well, we've got a fairly good idea where this came from, guv," put in Copper. "There's that gap in the cabinet in Sir Richard's library which looks spot-on for this, so we can pretty much rule out some mad maniac from Istanbul turning up, weapon in hand."

"Disregarding my sergeant's rather extravagant flight of fancy," remarked Constable drily to Singleton, "it does rather look as if the person who wielded the weapon took advantage of what was available on site rather than bringing it with them. Fair assessment?"

"Quite possibly, sir," replied Singleton. "We

examined the cabinet with all the other oriental bits and bobs in it, because we were thinking along the same lines as Sergeant Copper. But I'm afraid the only clear prints on it were those of Sir Richard himself."

"Hum. That's helpful. I can't see him stabbing himself in the chest, what with everything else that seems to have been going on. Right. Let's move on."

At that moment there came a tap at the door, and Singleton's young colleague entered with the tray bearing the coffee things, and proceedings came to a halt for a few moments while the police officers poured themselves a drink. But after a brief pause - "Feeling better, sergeant?" "Raring to go, guv." - the investigation resumed.

"I don't know if you've got this stuff in any particular sequence of importance, Singleton?" enquired the inspector.

"Not really, sir."

"In which case," suggested Constable, "having started in the centre of things with the body itself, let's work outwards. So what was nearest to our victim?"

"That would be this, sir." Singleton indicated a cut-glass tumbler. "It was on the victim's desk."

"An empty glass. Shall I make a note of that, guv?"

"Thank you, Copper. Flippant remarks are exactly what we need at a time like this."

"Sorry, guv."

"Do go on, Sergeant Singleton, and make an effort to ignore the heckling from the cheap seats."

"Of course, sir." The SOCO officer gave a small

smile which mingled suppressed amusement with a touch of sympathy for her colleague. "But, in fact, it's not the glass itself which is interesting, but what was in it. Which one of my colleagues finished analysing not long before you arrived."

"And these interesting contents would be ...?"

"There's whisky – I can't go so far as to tell you which brand, but it's definitely Scotch, single malt, and an un-peated variety. It's identical to a sample we took from a decanter in the drawing room."

"It's a classic whisky tumbler – no great surprises there. I'm guessing that the surprises are still to come."

"There was also some water, sir. It seems that the drinker liked a modest splash of water with his Scotch."

"And ...?" Constable raised an interrogative eyebrow.

Una Singleton took pity on the inspector. "And," she finished with an impish grin, "a dose of a rather potent raticide."

"You what?" asked Copper.

"Rat poison to you, David ... sergeant, I mean," replied Singleton.

Copper brightened. "Now that, guv, I am going to make a note of. That's as nice a classic method of doing away with someone as I've ever heard of."

"And you also might want to make a note," continued Singleton, "that it is also very often the murder weapon of choice in rural agricultural circles."

"You're kidding. How come?"

"It's actually one of the first things one of the old hands explained to me when I moved here and started getting involved with cases out in the sticks," explained Singleton. "If you think it through, it's really quite obvious. Wherever you have livestock, you have stores of feed for them. And there's nothing a rat likes more than a nice bulging feed store – it's like a rodent supermarket. So farmers have to use all sorts of methods to keep the little bug... little burglars out of their corn bins – traps, sticky panels, and those nice green plastic housings ..."

"... in which they place rat-bait," completed Constable. "Very neat."

"But Sir Richard wasn't a farmer," objected Copper.

"You're forgetting Punter," said the inspector. "Lady Olivia's horse. There's obviously a store for his oats somewhere near his stable, so I wouldn't mind betting that there would be some kind of anti-rat precautions in place. We'll check up on that when we're back at the house." He paused for a moment in thought. "And this glass was on Sir Richard's desk, you say?"

"That's right, sir."

"I remember Lady Olivia said something about the family gathering for drinks before dinner, guv. And then when Mrs. Wadsworth turned up, Mr. Pelham told Sir Richard, who then went through to the library. He must have taken his drink with him. We'd better ask Mr. Pelham how come the poison got into the whisky." Copper grinned. "Wow! I'd love it to be him. Wouldn't it be great to have a case where the butler actually did it?"

"Calm down, sergeant." Constable couldn't help himself smiling at his junior colleague's remark. "Before you get carried away, you ought to bear in mind that, according to Mr. Pelham himself, he never handled the family's drinks because they always did them for themselves. So you're going to have to find another culprit."

"Rats!" exclaimed Copper. "Sorry, guv ... that one came out by accident." He chuckled. "Mind you, guv, if Sir Richard was seen off by a dose of rat poison, it's not absolutely inappropriate, is it? I mean, if we believe what Mrs. Wadsworth told us, he was something of a love-rat, wasn't he?"

"Oh please, spare us the tabloid clichés," sighed Constable. He raised his eyes skywards and turned back to Una Singleton. "Shall at least some of us try to remain focussed? How about prints on the glass?"

"Several, sir," she replied. "We took the precaution of scanning everyone's in the house, chiefly for elimination purposes, should it be necessary. Sir Richard's, of course. And there were also some from the housekeeper, and from Lady Olivia and Mr. Booker-Gresham, but they could all quite possibly have come from simply touching or moving the glass. Sir Richard's were the ones that overlay all the others."

"And so the last one to handle the glass." The inspector gave a wry smile. "No doubt, in one of Copper's more fanciful scenarios, Sir Richard took a dose of poison and then, just to make sure, stabbed

130

himself in the chest." He sighed. "Right, moving on. What else do we have?"

"Now we're heading over to the fireplace, sir. And in the log-box alongside it, we found this." Singleton held up a clear plastic bag, in the corner of which could be seen nestling a slim and elegant cigarette lighter.

"Very smart," remarked Copper. "Gold?"

"It's hallmarked," confirmed Singleton. "And from a rather exclusive shop in the Burlington Arcade in London. And before you ask, yes, there are fingerprints."

"Do we know whose?"

"Not as yet. They don't tally with anyone in the house, but of course, we haven't had a chance yet to get through all the people who may be involved in the case."

"I'm prepared to hazard a wild guess as to whose it is," said Constable. "But what I can't guess is what it's doing in a library log-box."

"I don't think you'll need much in the way of guesswork when you see this, sir," said Singleton, indicating the next item on the table. Encased in plastic, the impressive formal document was printed on heavy cream paper in a typeface intended to resemble a flowing cursive script. The effect was grand and stately, marred only by the fact that the document finished abruptly halfway down with a line of burning.

"It's a will, guv," exclaimed Copper. "Which it looks as if someone has tried to destroy."

"I see your detectional skills are as finely honed as ever, sergeant," remarked the inspector.

"There's no slipping anything past you."

"Be nice to know what it says, guv. What with the fancy writing and the plastic, I can't make out a thing."

"We thought that might be a problem," smiled Singleton. "So, specially for Sergeant Copper, we made a copy of the contents." She handed over a sheet of typescript.

"Come along then, sergeant," said Constable. "What's it all about?" He leaned back against the table edge with an expectant expression on his face.

Dave Copper cleared his throat self-consciously. "Here goes, sir. *'This is the last will and testament of Richard James Jolyon Cavendish Effingham, Baronet, Member of the Most Noble Order of the British Empire, of Effingham Hall, Knaggs End, in the County of Wessex.'*"

"That's more like it. I do like a nice will in a murder case," commented the inspector. "Rich sources of motive, as a rule. Go on."

"*'I hereby revoke all earlier wills and testamentary dispositions.'*"

"Nothing unusual there."

"*'I hereby appoint as executor of this my will the senior partner at the time of my death of my legal advisors Messrs Cheetham and Partners, Solicitors and Commissioners for Oaths, of Knaggs End.'* That's interesting, guv. Do you suppose that could be this Miss Robson-Bilkes I haven't tracked down yet?"

"Could easily be, sergeant. Which gives you even more reason to speak to the lady."

"*'I direct that my debts shall be paid and my funeral expenses settled from my estate.'* Debts?

Wonder if that's significant, sir?"

"I doubt it. It's a perfectly normal provision, and we've had no hints that Sir Richard was in any kind of financial trouble. Carry on. Let's get to the meat of this thing."

"Righty-ho, guv. *'I give bequeath and devise the sum of two years' salary each, as payable at the date of my death or at the date of their leaving my employment, whichever shall be later, to my employees Edward John Pelham, Elspeth Mary Carruthers, and Elias Jeroboam Diggory in recognition of their long and faithful service to me and my family.'* That's quite generous of the old boy. I wouldn't mind if the Chief Constable popped off and left me two years' salary in his will." Copper grinned. "If he starts looking a bit peaky, do you suppose you could put in a word for me, sir?"

"I think the accent was on 'long and faithful service', Copper," replied Constable. "Which yours is unlikely to be if you don't get back to the point."

"Sorry, sir. Carrying on. *'I give bequeath and devise ...'*" Copper broke off. "How come they always have to say the same thing three times? Do you reckon it's all a ploy to bump up the lawyers' fees?" At a look from the inspector, he hastily resumed his reading. "... *'give bequeath and devise the sum of One Hundred Thousand Pounds Sterling each absolutely free of charges and inheritance taxes to Sarah Jane Wadsworth, to James Arbuthnot Booker-Gresham, and to Owen Elliott.'* Wow! Now that's meaty, if you like."

"At last," smiled the inspector. "Something that we can treat as a potential motive."

"And not just one, but three," pointed out Copper. "Or even six, if you count the servants."

"Yes. That doesn't exactly clarify matters. Although I'm pretty confident we can rule out the staff. They were all fairly well accounted for. But it does give us another line of investigation. So, what other nuggets are there?"

"Sorry, guv, but that's where it runs out. There's the start of another line beginning *'I give ...'*, but that's where it's burnt away. See, if you look at the original, you can see."

"Quite." Constable leaned over the document to examine it closely. "You can just make out the start of a word further along that line ... *'est...'* ... could be 'estate' but there's really no way of knowing. Singleton, I don't suppose you have any magical means of resurrecting the burnt portion in order to find out what it said?"

"Sorry, sir. Sometimes we can, but the remnants were too disintegrated to do anything with."

"A shame. It looks as if we might have been getting to the interesting parts. Not that what we've got isn't interesting. And highly suggestive, in some cases. Can we take this copy with us, Singleton? I think I need to sit down quietly and think about it."

"Of course, sir."

"In the meantime, what more do we have?"

"We're still in the library, sir. And the last thing we have is a dog lead. It was lying on the floor between Sir Richard's chair and the door to the hall."

Constable shrugged. "Any reason why it

should be of particular interest? We've met the dog. She seems an amiable enough old animal, so I'm assuming you haven't uncovered some reason why she would want her master dead. Plus, I seem to remember the butler mentioned that when Sir Richard returned from his afternoon walk, he had the dog lead with him when he went through to the library with Mr. Worcester. Isn't that right, Copper?"

"It is, sir," confirmed the sergeant. "That's what Mr. Pelham told us."

"It was something Dr. Livermore mentioned, sir," said Singleton. "I think it may have been as he was leaving, and he just tossed over his shoulder a remark about some marks around the victim's neck. We took some photos, and we also took the dog lead, just on the off-chance. It's a good job we did. The marks on Sir Richard's neck and the pattern of metal links on the lower portion of the lead match. I'd say it was a racing certainty that the lead was used in strangulation."

Constable grimaced. "Well, it's not a startling revelation. The doctor did canvass the possibility of that. Any information as to who had been handling the lead?"

"Far too much for comfort, sir. All the members of the family had handled it at some time or another, as well as the butler and the housekeeper. And everything is so jumbled that I doubt if I can give you any sort of time-line."

"Not to worry," sighed the inspector. "We'll have a confirmatory chat with Dr. Livermore. We're due to see him when we've finished here. So, moving on. What's next?"

"This, sir." Singleton held out a long thin object, encased in clear plastic wrap like its fellows.

Dave Copper let out a guffaw. "So that's what one of those looks like," he exclaimed in delight "I've always wondered. Cor, that takes me back."

Constable exchanged glances of amused bewilderment with Singleton. "Any chance of an explanation as to what on earth you're going on about, sergeant?" he asked mildly.

"It's a 'stick with an 'orse's 'ead 'andle', isn't it, guv," grinned Copper. "Just like the one in the old music hall poem."

Light dawned. "Oh, that. 'Albert and the Lion'. Good grief. I haven't heard that for years. Stanley Holloway, wasn't it, if I recall correctly? Isn't that all a bit before your time?"

"Maybe so, guv, but whenever our family all got together – you know, Christmases and so on – my grandad always used to recite the poem to all of us kids. It was kind of his party piece. You know, I bet I could still remember most of it."

Constable turned to Singleton. "I always suspected Sergeant Copper would regress to his childhood, given half a chance," he murmured in an aside which made no attempt at discretion. "However, in the here and now, we appear to have an item which somehow relates to a murder enquiry, so let's all be a little more serious." He regarded the object. "Right. Clearly a walking stick. Wood – couldn't guess at what sort, but I don't suppose that is relevant anyway – topped with a silver handle in the shape of a horse's head. Are those hallmarks I can see?"

"Yes, sir," confirmed Singleton.

"So, solid silver. A valuable item. Not, presumably, 'the finest that Woolworth's could sell'. And we've heard mention of a walking stick before in our various conversations, so I'm assuming that this is the property of the late Sir Richard. You've checked?" A nod. "Why is it here?"

"It was something that was mentioned when we were at the house, sir. I can't remember offhand who said it – it might have been the butler – but anyway, the dog lead and the walking stick were somehow referred to in the same sentence."

"I remember that too, guv," interjected Copper. "Mr. Pelham said Sir Richard took the lead and the walking stick when he went out with the dog. And didn't he say that it turned up in the hall stand later?"

"He did," said Constable. "I recall saying we'd look into that. It seems our SOCO friends beat us to the punch."

"It was just an instinct, sir." Singleton smiled in self-deprecation. "I always remember what you told me in that case at the theatre. 'Never disregard that itch at the back of your brain,' you said. And this was one of those itches."

"Which you felt compelled to scratch?" smiled the inspector. "And the result was ...?"

"Blood, sir. Deep in the crevices of the moulding of the horse's head. Not much, and there had been an obvious attempt to clean it all off, but there was enough."

"Enough to identify whose? I'm guessing we can all work out the answer to that."

"Quite right, sir. It was Sir Richard's. Other than that, there's not a lot I can tell you. And, of course, the cleaning has wiped away any traces which might have indicated who last handled it."

"I think we can reasonably suppose that it wasn't Sir Richard himself. It looks pretty clear to me that here we have the famous blunt instrument which the doctor spoke of. Used to deliver that nasty wound to the victim's head."

"I'm going to take another closer look at it myself under a microscope, sir," said Singleton. "Just in case there's anything my team have missed."

"Let me know if you find anything. And it looks as if we're coming to the end of our list."

"We are, sir. Just one item left. And here it is."

"More silver," remarked Constable. "A hip flask. Just the sort of thing you'd want to take with you when you go walking the dog on a crisp winter's day. Which this wasn't, but let's not split hairs. Also Sir Richard's?"

"We think not, sir. You're looking at the back. Turn it over."

Constable did so. Engraved in an escutcheon, in a proud gothic script, were the letters *'O.E'*. "I see what you mean. Obviously not the dead man's initials. Has this been shown to anyone in the house?"

"The butler, sir, and the gardener. They both said they didn't recognise it."

"But the initials, sir," broke in Copper. "Bit of a give-away, aren't they? 'O.E.' - surely that's got to be Owen Elliott."

Constable smiled. "Has it, sergeant? Has it

really? That's the only 'O.E.' you can think of in the case?"

Copper looked baffled for a few moments, but then slapped himself on the forehead. "D'oh! Sorry, guv – being dense. There's also Lady Olivia – Olivia Effingham. But surely it's got to be one of those two."

"Just a couple of flaws in your thinking," replied the inspector. "One, Owen Elliott told us he didn't drink. We can check with the local pub, of course – they would most likely know one way or the other – but alcohol is a great way of putting on weight, whereas most jockeys are more concerned with getting weight off. Just a thought. And as for her ladyship, this isn't a particularly ladylike item, is it? Far too masculine to be tucked into a lady's handbag or whatever. So I suspect we will need to continue to think about this flask." A pause as a thought struck him. "Hold on a second, Singleton. You haven't told us why we're thinking about it in the first place. What's peculiar about it?"

"Not so much what as where, sir. It was found by one of the team in one of the flowerbeds outside the library windows. There are still some odd little traces of earth sticking to it, if you look closely, from where it was most probably dropped. And there were also footprints in that same flowerbed, but before you get your hopes up, I have to say that they were so badly scuffed that it wasn't possible to tell much about them other than that the footwear was almost definitely male. Maybe some sort of boot."

"Gardener's wellies?" hazarded Copper. "Wouldn't that be logical?"

"With Lady Effingham on the warpath about her precious borders, I can't see Diggory trying to get away with that. But we'll check with him anyway. Hmmm." A wry smile. "Not making this easy for us, are they?" he commented to his junior colleague. "How about contents, Singleton?"

"Whisky, sir," she said. "Single malt, exactly the same type as was found in Sir Richard's glass."

"As if we needed any more confusing coincidences," grumped Constable.

"But," continued Singleton, "there may be more to tell. If whoever's flask this is took a swig from it directly, there may be some DNA to be recovered from around the neck. We're working on that."

"How old is it? Is it an antique?" queried Copper. "You never know, guv. It might be relevant."

"Sorry to disappoint," said Singleton. "It's modern, according to the hallmarks. Made about twenty-five years ago. But not cheap, for all that. It's got the maker's mark for a very smart shop in London. Holders of the Royal Warrant, no less."

"Not by any remote chance the same source as the cigarette lighter?" said Constable hopefully.

"Sadly not, sir," smiled the SOCO officer. "I can't offer you that interesting coincidence."

"I always find coincidences greatly over-rated in a murder enquiry," said Constable. "They're often more trouble than they're worth. But thanks anyway." He checked his watch. "Good grief. This has all taken rather longer than I thought. I think we'd better make our escape and go and track down Dr. Livermore before he gets hauled out again on some other matter. Thank you for all that, Singleton, and please keep me posted if you get any further results."

"Of course, sir. Goodbye." A sparkle returned to her eyes. "Goodbye, David ... sergeant."

Chapter 10

"Good morning, doctor."

"Is it?" Dr. Livermore looked up from the workbench where he appeared to be engaged in handing over a variety of surgical equipment to a rather nervous-looking and rabbity junior colleague. "Not if you've been dragging some poor old lady out of her grave in order to find out whether one of your esteemed colleagues has let the entire profession in for another session of being comprehensively berated by the media, it isn't. And now I have to write a long and tedious report which will probably ensure that some half-witted idiot who should probably never have been allowed to practice in the first place will get struck off, to the great delight of the chattering classes. So, Inspector Constable, you do not find me in the sunniest of moods!"

"Sorry to hear that, doctor."

"And another thing, inspector. I do not appreciate being badgered to produce my findings concerning Sir Richard Effingham in double-quick time."

Andy Constable did a double-take. "Sorry, doctor. I don't know what you mean."

The doctor raised a doubting eyebrow. "The word came down from on high that it would be appreciated if I would let the coroner have my findings as soon as possible, so that the inquest could be arranged without delay. I assumed that must have been something to do with you."

Constable exchanged glances with Dave Copper. "Nothing to do with me, doctor. Copper, get

142

on the phone. See if you can find out what's going on."

"Righty-ho, guv." Copper obediently pulled his phone from his pocket.

"Not in here, laddie, if you don't mind," snapped the doctor. "There is nothing more calculated to send up my blood pressure than listening to half of a conversation on a mobile telephone, usually of the 'I'm on the train' variety. So, out in the corridor, if you please."

"Certainly, doctor," replied Copper. "I'd hate to be responsible for your blood pressure causing any problems. We don't want you ending up prematurely on one of your own slabs, do we?" The cheery grin faded from his face in response to the stony looks directed at him from the other two men. "I'll ... I'll be outside then, guv." He scuttled for the door.

"Forgive Sergeant Copper's misplaced sense of humour, doctor," said Constable. "I've had a great deal of practice coping with it, but it does come as a surprise to some people. Anyway, while he's engaged on the phone, why don't we make a start with Sir Richard? Where is he? And have you got anything new to show me?"

"I haven't got anything to show you at all," retorted the doctor grumpily. "If you want to see the body, you're too late. It's gone."

"Gone? Gone where?"

"Passed into the custody of the Effingham family's usual funeral directors, I understand." And as Constable opened his mouth to object, "Don't look at me. Matter taken out of my hands. As I said, the

143

word came down from on high. Your sergeant may be able to tell you how high. But don't worry – I've got all my results noted down, even if I haven't had a chance to codify them formally, and there's an embargo on doing anything with the body until after the inquest."

Constable sighed. "So, can you tell me what we do know?"

Dr. Livermore softened slightly. "You'd better come into my office and sit down. I've got my notes in there." He led the way away from the harsh glare of fluorescent lighting and gleaming hard surfaces into a small side office, surprisingly cosy with wood panelling dotted with framed certificates and what appeared to be family photographs, comfortable tub chairs upholstered in dark red leather, and soft lighting. "My sanctum away from the cruel realities of death," he commented. "Take a seat while I find the file." He opened a laptop and clicked some keys.

"I've just come from speaking to Sergeant Singleton from the SOCO team," said Constable while the doctor searched for his records. "I think she has more or less confirmed many of the things you were originally suggesting when we spoke at the scene."

"I should hope so too," retorted Livermore. "Just because we're rather better off for trees and fields over on this side of the county, that doesn't mean we're all country bumpkins, you know. I've been doing this long enough to know what I'm about."

"I'm sure you have, doctor," soothed Constable. "But I never mind going for the belt-and-braces approach when it's a case of putting facts before a jury."

"Ah. Here we are. So, let's see ..."

"Could we perhaps start with the most obvious of the wounds to the body, doctor?" suggested the inspector. "The dagger."

"Right to the heart of the matter, eh?" Livermore gave an unexpected twinkle. "Which in actual fact it was. Blade sharp as you please, probably slipped in with little or no effort, and I've got the measurements of the penetration here which no doubt somebody will want to tally with the actual dimensions of what SOCO have, but I think we can both agree that there's no dispute about what we're talking about and where it was found. Very little blood, though. That's one thing I've been scratching my head over."

"Maybe the stab to the heart was so effective that death was instantaneous," hazarded Constable. "Could that have stopped the blood flow immediately? Of course," he admitted, "I don't really have the faintest idea of what I'm talking about."

"It's not the most stupid suggestion I've ever heard," responded the doctor. "But I'm still thinking about that."

"And while we're thinking about blood, doctor, Sergeant Singleton showed me Sir Richard's walking stick which had been found to have traces of blood on it. Confirmed as his."

"Yes. We did have an enquiry regarding that. And it all tallied."

"So do we conclude therefore that the stick is the most likely instrument to have caused the head wound you showed me?"

"Most probably," agreed the doctor with a touch of reluctance. "I would have been happier if there had been any hair or skin attached to be absolutely certain of a match, but you can't have everything. I gather there had been some sort of ham-fisted attempt to remove any incriminating traces, but the criminals would have to get up very early in the morning to slip anything past your Sergeant Singleton." A smile. "She's a bright young woman, but don't let her know I said so. I always prefer to keep all the SOCO people in a state of mild terror. It helps to ensure that they try their utmost not to miss anything."

"My lips are sealed, doctor," said Constable with an answering smile. He felt himself beginning to warm to the dry humour which seemed to lurk beneath Livermore's forbidding exterior. "Another thing which she showed me was the dog lead which was lying on the library floor. Apparently it accords perfectly with what you told us regarding the marks around Sir Richard's neck."

"Can't say I'm surprised," said the doctor. "Thought it might have been something of the kind, but I didn't want to lead your people by the nose too much. I've got some thoughts on the implications of that, which are probably rather too technical to go into here and now, but I'll develop them in my report so you can absorb them at your leisure. So now, unless you have any questions, we'll move on to the next thing, which is the shooting."

"Which was, of course, the last thing to take place, and the event which alerted the whole household to the situation. What have you been able discover?"

"In the absence of the gun itself – I'm assuming you don't have it ...?"

"It hasn't been found so far, but the search is still under way. But I imagine that won't have stopped you finding out a certain amount."

"Not at all. We managed to dig quite a few pellets out of your dead man." The inspector gulped slightly at the doctor's words. "Perfectly ordinary lead pellets from a perfectly standard 12-bore shotgun. The sort you'll probably find on nine farms out of ten in the English countryside. And probably also in its sawn-off incarnation in quite a few of the nastier parts of our big cities, but we won't go into that. We'll stick to what we know, which is, that from the spread of the shot, I'm estimating that the gun was fired from approximately ten feet away from the victim."

Constable did a quick mental calculation. "I'm trying to visualise where in the room that would put the shooter."

"Can't help you there. I was rather too preoccupied with the body to be thinking very much about architectural details."

"And the wounds from the shotgun pellets? We're all assuming that they would have been fatal, since Sir Richard was obviously dead when he was discovered."

"He was certainly peppered with a considerable amount of shot. But don't forget, inspector, that you can bring down a pheasant with a single pellet," was the doctor's slightly evasive reply. "Anyway, there you have it, for what it's

147

worth. I've done a brief résumé for the coroner's office, which they seemed to think was satisfactory for their immediate needs. I'll spell everything out in a great deal more detail in my formal report, but that's all so far on the four various attempts on your dead man."

"Actually, doctor, it's five."

"What are you talking about, man?" bristled Livermore. "You saw the body as well as I did. I hope you're not suggesting that I've missed something."

"Not at all, doctor," replied Constable hastily. "This is something I didn't find out about myself until this morning. It was something that SOCO had found. I'm surprised they haven't communicated it to you."

"There was some garbled message that somebody took about checking for toxins. I ignored it because that is what we would normally do anyway. And you'll be getting a highly detailed list of stomach contents, if that sort of thing appeals to you. SOCO are quite welcome to a copy. What, do they think we don't know our job down here?" The doctor's heightened colour seemed to indicate that his blood pressure might be rising towards previously-mentioned hazardous levels.

"I'm sure that's not the case, doctor." Constable made a strenuous effort to pour oil on troubled waters. "I expect it's just a question of belt-and-braces again. It's just that you haven't mentioned the matter."

"No reason why I should," said Livermore. "So what are SOCO saying?"

"They showed me a whisky glass which was

on Sir Richard's desk," explained the inspector. "They'd analysed the contents, and apparently it contained a significant dose of rat poison."

"What? Ridiculous!"

"I assure you, doctor, that is what Sergeant Singleton told me. And as you pointed out, she is a very bright young woman. I'm sure SOCO would have been unlikely to make a mistake over such a thing."

"Well, you can tell SOCO from me that, in this instance, they're barking up the wrong tree. There might have been poison in the glass, but I'll stake my reputation on the fact that Sir Richard never touched it. There wasn't a trace of any toxin present in his body."

*

Back out in the corridor, Andy Constable encountered a nervously-hovering Dave Copper. "What are you doing lurking out here, sergeant?"

"I thought I'd better not risk Doctor Livermore's wrath by coming back in, guv. I'm not sure he and I are on the same wavelength, and I didn't want to get in your way."

"Probably wise."

"Any startling revelations, sir?"

"Not really. A few more details about the injuries we already knew about, but the whole thing is going to be laid out for me in considerable detail in the doctor's report, so it looks as if I shall have the exquisite pleasure of ploughing through that in due course."

"And we all know how fond you are of paperwork," said Copper in sympathetic tones.

"But it has to be done," sighed Constable. "Oh. One thing did turn out to be startling, but it was the doctor on the receiving end of the surprise. He knew nothing about the poison in Sir Richard's glass, and he was adamant that there was no trace of any such thing in his body."

"So there's another scenario we can rule out, guv. Sir Richard definitely didn't poison himself before not hitting himself over the head and then not stabbing himself in the chest. You know, I'm beginning to think that this suicide theory of ours is never going to hold water."

Constable laughed in spite of himself. "Copper, you can sometimes be a complete idiot. But that's probably what it takes to keep me sane." He resumed a serious demeanour. "Back to business. What did you manage to find out about this business with the coroner?"

"It's all a bit odd, sir," replied Copper. "Everyone's being rather tight-lipped, but I get the impression that things are being pushed through on a fast track in order to minimise any possible embarrassment in certain quarters. Nobody will say anything specific, but I got hints that it may have something to do with the fact that Sir Richard was married to an earl's daughter, and the earl may or may not be long-standing chums with the Home Secretary's father. Oh, there's no hint of a cover-up," he added hastily as the inspector seemed to be about to interrupt. "It's just that I think they want everything tidied away as quickly as possible. And the long and short of it is that the inquest has been scheduled for first thing tomorrow morning."

"Hell's teeth," retorted Constable. "That's pushing on a bit. But, I suppose, nothing untoward. We've had quick inquests before. I imagine it will be the short version – formal identification, details of the event to follow in due course."

"That's what it sounds like sir."

"So what else have you been doing to occupy your time? I assume you haven't just been lurking out here doing nothing."

"Far from it, guv. In fact, I've actually achieved some progress. I managed to get in touch with Susan Robson-Bilkes."

"You succeeded in tracking down our elusive solicitor? Well done, you. And ...?"

"The lady didn't want to talk on the phone, sir. But she has graciously deigned to give us some moments of her time at her office this afternoon."

"How very grand of her. I get the impression that you and Miss Robson-Bilkes did not entirely hit it off."

"A bit snooty for my taste, sir. I think she fancies herself as a bit of a dragon. Didn't really want to talk to an underling. I think only an inspector is good enough for her."

Constable raised an eyebrow. "Thank goodness she'll settle for me. Otherwise we could have faced the prospect of dragging the Chief Superintendent into the case, which, knowing her, would not have helped matters one little bit. And you did not hear me say that."

"Say what, sir?" grinned Copper.

The inspector looked at his watch. "Approaching lunchtime. I think, sergeant, that it would be a very good idea if we were to head over in the direction of Knaggs End and take a spot of lunch at the Four Horseshoes. I noticed some rather enticing venison sausages on their menu when we were last there, so I think it would be a good plan to check out whether they are as good as they sound."

"You'll get no arguments from me, guv," smiled the sergeant.

"And we shall then be very handily placed for our little chat with your new solicitor friend. Right. Onwards and upwards. Or rather, downwards to the car park." Constable headed for the stairs.

*

As he used the final portion of creamy mash to soak up the last remnants of the rich red wine and onion gravy which had accompanied his venison sausages, Andy Constable leaned back with a satisfied sigh. "You know, Copper, I think Sergeant Singleton had the right idea, getting herself transferred to this neck of the woods. The catering here is so much better than the unappetising mush they dish up in the station canteen."

"Or even the pie and chips they do across the road in the Collar and Cuffs," agreed Dave Copper. "They obviously don't know what real pub food is."

Constable smiled. "If we're not careful, we shall find ourselves offering to contribute a food critic's column for the next edition of the county police magazine."

"Ah, but we have other fish to fry, guv."

Constable groaned. "That's it. One bad Copper joke too many. Back to work, I think."

The front door of the premises of Cheetham

and Partners was opened by a timid-looking bespectacled waif with a sniff. In response to Constable's 'Detective Inspector Constable and Detective Sergeant Copper to see Miss Robson-Bilkes, please. I believe she's expecting us', she stepped back into the hall, standing aside to allow the detectives to enter, and then disappeared wordlessly through an adjacent door, from which a murmur of conversation could then be heard.

"She says come in," she squeaked, before scuttling back to her place behind a desk in a corner of the entrance hall.

Susan Robson-Bilkes rose from behind an impressive partners' desk as the detectives entered her office. Bookcases, glass-fronted and filled with leather-bound volumes, many looking to be of a considerable vintage, occupied the wall behind her. Portraits of solemn and sober-suited gentlemen in Georgian costume and Victorian frock coats hung above the stately marble fireplace and adorned the other walls. A mahogany sofa table held a silver tray bearing several gleaming decanters and their accompanying cut-crystal glasses. A chesterfield in dark brown leather lounged beneath the bay sash windows, while matching armchairs were arranged in front of the desk. The general effect was very much that of an Edwardian gentleman's library.

"Good afternoon, inspector." The voice was low-pitched. Susan Robson-Bilkes was tall and thin, with jet-black hair cut in a jaw-length bob which did nothing to soften the angular planes of her face. Her eyes, beneath sharply delineated brows, were dark, and held no warmth. Her nose was long and almost

153

seemed to come to a point. Her mouth was a thin scarlet slash. She wore a severe black business suit, almost unrelieved except for the merest touch of white at the throat. "I've been told you wish to speak to me." The words held no acknowledgement of the involvement, or even the presence, of Dave Copper.

The inspector smiled blandly. "Indeed I do, Miss Robson-Bilkes. On the matter of the late Sir Richard Effingham, as I'm sure you know. I wonder, might we sit down?" He looked expectantly at the armchairs positioned before the desk and, in response to a wintery nod, took a seat. As the solicitor resumed her place behind her desk, Copper likewise seated himself and produced his notebook, preparing to record any relevant information.

Susan finally condescended to notice the junior officer and frowned disapprovingly. "I don't think I can allow your sergeant to make notes, inspector. You may be asking questions which might lead to privileged information emerging." The look on her face clearly indicated doubts.

"No matter, Miss Robson-Bilkes." Constable waved to Copper to put away his notebook. "I'm sure we can manage very well without. And in any case, Sergeant Copper has an excellent memory." Another smile, this one more wolfish in nature.

"So, how can I help you?"

"Just to confirm a few basic facts, to begin with. You were Sir Richard's solicitor?"

"I was. And, to be strictly accurate, still am."

"As the executor of his will?"

A blink of surprise. "As it happens, yes. Although I'm not at all sure how you would have come by that particular piece of information."

"Perhaps we'll come on to that a little later. But you have, I understand, been involved in Sir Richard's affairs for many years."

"The legal affairs?" A flare of the nostrils, whose meaning Constable did not immediately understand. "Those, yes. In fact, this firm has been handling the family's legal business since Sir Richard's ancestor built the Hall."

"Although I think there may have been something of a ... shall we say, a hiccup in the relationship some little while ago?"

A small gleam of alarm showed in Susan's eyes. "I really don't know what you mean, inspector."

"Oh, I think perhaps you do, Miss Robson-Bilkes," contradicted Constable. "We both know that hearsay will get us nowhere in a legal context, but my colleague and I have been told certain things which I have no cause to doubt. Something to do with the contents of one of Sir Richard's books, I believe."

"I really ..."

"'Murder For The Defence' was the title, I think," pressed on Constable. He waited.

Susan capitulated. "Yes, inspector," she said shortly. "There was a ... misunderstanding."

"You took exception to one of the characters, I'm told. A lady lawyer."

"It was a storm in a teacup." Susan essayed a light laugh which did not ring true. "There were things in the book which could quite easily have been misinterpreted. Once these were pointed out,

155

the whole matter was swiftly resolved."

"Without recourse to the law."

"As you say, inspector." Susan did not seem disposed to be any more forthcoming.

"And to your entire satisfaction?" persisted the inspector.

The solicitor's hackles began to rise. "I fail to see what you are attempting to imply, Mr. Constable," she said frostily. "There was a disagreement between Sir Richard and myself on a certain topic. The disagreement ended, and as you appear to be aware, I have continued to act for him with regard to legal matters, so I assume you will deduce that the resolution was complete and amicable."

"Sir Richard's skills of persuasion certainly seem to have been finely polished," commented Constable, and hurried on before Susan could raise any objection to the remark. "Now, you confirm that you continued to act for Sir Richard. This would be true in regard to his will, of course?"

"This is the second time you have referred to Sir Richard's will, inspector. And I'm sure I do not need to remind you that you are treading perilously close to matters of client confidentiality."

"Under normal circumstances, naturally," agreed Constable. "But I'm sure I do not need to remind you, Miss Robson-Bilkes, that these circumstances are very far from normal. I am investigating the murder of your client. And in such circumstances, something like a will can be very relevant where matters of inheritance are concerned. There are potential motives to be looked into. And in this instance, I have a particular reason for raising the matter. You see, we have in our possession a copy of Sir Richard's will."

"What?" Susan was clearly startled. "Where … I mean, how …?"

"As to where, I can simply say that it was at the crime scene. How is still a matter of some speculation. But what would be helpful to know, Miss Robson-Bilkes, is whether this is the latest will which Sir Richard made, and if so, when he made it."

"But if you have the will," said Susan slowly, "then surely you don't need me to give you that information."

"Sadly, the document in our possession is incomplete." Constable declined to give any further details. "But I hope you may be able to give us some guidance." Susan's face took on an expression of defiance. "Merely as a professional courtesy, naturally. Of course. I could roust out a magistrate and go through the rigmarole of getting authority to view the will, but I would hate to put you to all the inconvenience. And it goes without saying that I wouldn't expect you to reveal anything of a confidential nature."

Susan sighed. "Oh, very well," she said reluctantly. "I certainly shan't tell you any of the detailed provisions of the will …"

"Of some of which, we are already aware."

"If you say so, inspector. Provided that the one you have is the most recent, of course," she retorted waspishly. "And that was made some two weeks ago, here in this office. I recall the occasion well. And it was witnessed by my receptionist and one of the filing clerks from records. That is all I am prepared to reveal until the will is read formally."

"Which is likely to be when?"

"Under normal circumstances, immediately following Sir Richard's funeral."

"Then we may not have to wait too long. There is an inquest being held tomorrow ..."

"Tomorrow?"

"Surprisingly soon, wouldn't you say? I believe there have been pressures, but I won't bore you with those. So if all goes well, it may be possible to arrange the funeral in the near future. At which time, we shall all become much better informed."

Chapter 11

"Charming helpful lady, isn't she, guv?" remarked Dave Copper as the detectives returned to their car. "Eager to tell us all she knows in the interests of the pursuit of justice."

"Do I detect the merest hint that you may be becoming jaded, sergeant?" responded Andy Constable with a smile.

"Not even a touch, sir. Mind you, I'll tell you one thing. I would love it if she were one of our suspects. I reckon some awkward questions in the interview room would wipe some of that sneer off her face."

"Don't let it get personal, David," warned Constable. "Just because the lady treated you like some kind of pond life. There are some of us who appreciate your sterling qualities." A pause, and a quiet chuckle. "Just don't ask me to enumerate them."

"Well, thanks for that, guv," grinned Copper. "I think. Although, if you think about it, we could probably make a decent case for her having some kind of motive. There's all this kerfuffle over the book. And, don't you remember, when we were talking to Ed Short, I think he dropped some kind of hint that Miss Robson-Bilkes might have fancied her chances of joining Sir Richard's stable of fillies. I didn't think anything of it at the time he said it, and having clapped eyes on her, I can't see it myself, but there's no accounting for taste. But if he fobbed her off with a car and a share in a horse, tasty though those might be, she could still have felt miffed. She might have wanted to bump him off out of spite – you know, revenge being a dish best eaten cold, and all that."

Constable laughed. "Another one of your flights of fancy, sergeant. Which I very much enjoy, but I can't see that it will go anywhere. For one thing, there is nothing to place her anywhere near the house at the time of Sir Richard's death, and considering the number of people who were to-ing and fro-ing that evening, I'm sure she'd have been noticed. No, I'm afraid you will have to let that one go." He fumbled in his pocket for his keys as the two reached the car.

"So, what next then, guv?" asked Copper, climbing in.

"As we're in this neck of the woods, I think we'd best see if we can catch the housekeeper up at the Hall. She's about the only material witness we haven't yet spoken to, and there are one or two things raised by SOCO and the doctor that I'd rather like to clarify." Constable let in the clutch and pulled out of the Four Horseshoes car park on to the main road.

*

"I'm afraid Mrs. Carruthers is not here this afternoon, sir," said Pelham as he stood in the front doorway. "She always uses one of her half-days off to take the bus and go and see her sister in Westchester. May I be of help to you?"

"I don't think so, Mr. Pelham," said Constable. "I wanted to ask her about the events of the evening of Sir Richard's death as she saw them, and you've already been more than helpful on that front."

160

"She will most probably be back at around nine o'clock this evening, sir," suggested Pelham.

"I think perhaps tomorrow might be more convenient," replied Constable, his mind on a number of recent memos from the top brass on the subject of excessive payments for officers' overtime. "We'll speak to her then."

"I shall advise her to expect you, sir," said Pelham gravely.

As the detectives descended the steps from the front door, the squeak of a wheelbarrow caught their ear, and Diggory emerged around the corner of the house from the west terrace.

A thought struck the inspector. "Ah, Mr. Diggory," he cried. "Just the man."

The gardener lowered the handles of his barrow and straightened with a slight groan. "Oh, it's you, inspector," he said. "What is it you're after? 'Cos if it's about that gun, I don't know no more than I've already told you ..."

"Nothing to do with that, Mr. Diggory," said Constable. "I think we've already made our thoughts clear on that subject. No, this is something else that has emerged since we had our last conversation."

"Oh, what's that, then?" asked Diggory warily.

"Our colleagues on the forensic team have shown us a hip flask which was apparently found in one of the borders outside the house. I wonder if you can show us where it was."

"Oh, that. That's just round here." Diggory led the officers around the side of the house. "It was here, in this border."

"Is that the library though there?" asked

Copper, peering in through the window.

"It is, sergeant. Why?"

"Oh, I just wondered. Because I think I made a note that you told us that you saw Lady Effingham doing something in one of these borders on the day of Sir Richard's death. Would that have been this border?"

"That's right. And before you ask, it couldn't have been her who left those ruddy great footprints in there. She's got a bit more respect for my work than that. Course, I've put it all to rights now." Diggory indicated a freshly-trowelled area. "But if it wasn't the police, tramping all over the place in their great size 11s, I'd like to know who it was."

"And you've seen the flask," resumed Constable. "You're certain that it could not have belonged to her ladyship? After all, it does seem that it was engraved with her initials."

"That don't mean nothing," scoffed Diggory. "Plenty of people with them initials about. And anyway, it's no sort of a thing for a lady to have."

"You may be right." Constable elected to move on. "One other thing, Mr. Diggory. Tell me, do you keep rat poison?"

"Rat poison?" responded the gardener in surprise. "What would I want with rat poison? Weed killer, yes, I got some of that, and slug bait, 'cos some of those little blighters have got a terrible taste for succulents, not to mention my marrows. But I don't get any bother from rats."

"So there wouldn't be likely to be any rat poison on the premises?" The inspector sounded disappointed.

"Ah. No. I didn't say that."

"Then what did you say?" asked Constable, exasperated.

"You asked me if *I* keep it, and I don't. I believe there is some, but it ain't nothing to do with me. It's kept in the feed store, to keep the rats away from Punter's oats. They soaks a handful of oats in it, see, and puts them down in some out-of-the-way corner for the rats to eat."

"Which is exactly what you said, guv, when Sergeant Singleton told us what she'd found. Great – now we've got another suspect – Lady Olivia's horse!"

"Hack."

"Come again?" was Copper's baffled reaction.

"Apparently that's what they call a horse that's kept for ordinary everyday riding," explained Constable. "I've been doing some reading up."

"So if Punter was responsible for the murder, you could say ..." spluttered Copper in mirth. "... you could say Sir Richard had been hacked to death!"

"Pay no attention, Mr. Diggory," said Constable severely. "Just another of my sergeant's frequent misplaced attempts at humour. So, could you show us where this rat poison is kept?"

"Round here in the stable yard, inspector." Diggory led the way through a gate at the corner of the house and into the rear yard, opened the door of a storeroom next to the stable, and pointed to a bottle on a shelf full of dusty bottles above the bin of oats, alongside a rack of hay. Constable observed a small circular area on the shelf, noticeably clear of dust. Punter, alerted by the sounds coming from the

163

adjacent store, put his head out inquisitively from his stable, evidently in the hope of an extra unscheduled meal.

"And this door is not kept locked, I suppose," sighed Constable.

"No reason why it should be, is there?" said the gardener.

The inspector measured the distance to the door to the kitchen corridor with his eye. "And only a few yards from the house. Which means that anyone might have access."

"You'll have to ask Mrs. Carruthers about that," said Diggory. "She'd know more about the comings and goings through the kitchen than I would."

"And we shall do that very thing. Tomorrow. Come along, Copper. I think we're done here." Constable started back in the direction of the car. "As I believe someone once said, tomorrow is another day."

"I think it was you, sir," grinned Copper. "You want to watch out. They say repeating yourself is one of the first signs of madness."

"And for that, sergeant," riposted Constable, tossing across the keys to his junior colleague, "you can drive back to the station while I have a well-deserved snooze."

*

"Morning, guv."

Andy Constable looked up from the computer screen in front of him. "You're exceptionally chipper this morning, sergeant."

"Had a good night last night, sir," replied

Dave Copper. "I ran into Pete and Matt as I was going off work. They asked me what I was working on, and I told them about the case, and they accidentally reminded me that I'd promised to stand them a meal on the strength of my winnings on race day. So we went out and had a couple of lagers and some very fine chicken piri-piri."

"As long as the chilli hasn't killed off too many of your brain cells," remarked Constable. "I suppose there is always an outside chance that we may need to call on some of them this morning."

"So what's afoot then, guv?"

Constable turned back to the computer screen. "I was just checking what time the inquest on Sir Richard is scheduled to take place."

"Did you want to go then, sir?"

"I had it in mind to. Not, I suppose, that it is likely to tell us a great deal that we don't know already, given that we've spoken to Dr. Livermore and SOCO. But you never know, the coroner might want to ask the odd question, so it would do no harm to be on the spot, just in case."

"Where are they holding it?"

"One of the Westchester Magistrates Courts. Which is very convenient for going on to Effingham Hall and our proposed conversation with Mrs. Carruthers."

"Better saddle up and be on our way then, sir."

Constable sighed as he got to his feet. "You will run out of these remarks at some point, I hope, sergeant?"

"I wouldn't count on it, sir," grinned Copper.

"And I haven't even got to the one about Mr. Diggory not locking the stable door ..."

*

The proceedings at the virtually deserted inquest could scarcely have been briefer. Formal evidence of identification was given in just a few words, and a brief recitation was made of the injuries to the body. The conclusion went through on the nod.

"'Unlawful killing by person or persons unknown'," quoted Dave Copper, as the detectives climbed back into the car. "I could have told them that and saved them the trouble. It was hardly worth even sitting down. No help at all."

"On the contrary," said Andy Constable. "At least one thing has been achieved. The body has been released for burial, which means we get a funeral, which means we get to hear the full details of the will."

"And you reckon that's going to help?"

Constable shrugged. "Maybe not. But there may be a few extra facts which might add to the sum total of our knowledge."

"If my notebook is anything to go by, guv," returned Copper, "we're drowning in facts. My handwriting is getting smaller and smaller. And if we're off to see this housekeeper woman, you can bet she'll pile a few more facts on."

"And eventually they will form a pattern," said Constable. "Have faith, sergeant. Whatever happened to that power of positive thinking you always used to go on about?"

"It's suffering from writer's cramp, guv."

"Then you'd better start wiggling your fingers in anticipation, because it's not going to take very long to get to Effingham Hall." Constable started the car.

"You'll be wishing to speak to Mrs. Carruthers, I assume, gentlemen?" said Pelham as he answered the front door.

"We would," confirmed Constable.

"If you would care to step inside, inspector, I will fetch her for you. Perhaps my sitting room would be convenient ..."

"Oh, please don't put yourself to any trouble, Mr. Pelham," interrupted Constable. "We'll go to her. If you could just point us in the right direction ..." The detectives passed through the indicated maroon baize door at the foot of the stairs and found themselves in a short corridor, at the end of which, alongside a door which evidently led out to the stable yard, was an open door, through which floated the sound of a rather erratic soprano rendering of 'We'll Gather Lilacs'. Constable tapped on the door and went in.

A short grey-haired dumpling of a woman looked up from where she was arranging a batch of scones on a baking tray. "Just give me a moment to get these into the oven," she said and, suiting the action to the word, bent down to place the tray into a neat modern gas cooker which looked quite intimidated by the cavernous old-fashioned cast-iron range alongside it. Straightening, she wiped her hands on a cloth, carefully set a timer on the kitchen table, and removed the apron she wore, to reveal a neat and unfussy grey blouse above a plain black skirt and extremely sensible shoes. "Can I help you?" she enquired, in a brisk Scots accent.

"Do all housekeepers have to be Scottish?" murmured Copper in an aside to his superior. "Is it the law?"

Constable ignored him. "You'll be Mrs. Carruthers, I take it?"

"That's right, sir. Elspeth Carruthers. And you'll be the police gentlemen Mr. Pelham said would be calling, no doubt."

"We are. Detective Inspector Constable and Detective Sergeant Copper." The two offered their warrant cards for perusal. "And as I'm sure you've been told, we'd like your help in answering some questions about the events on the day of Sir Richard's death."

"Of course, inspector. It's all very sad. Anything I can do. Won't you sit down? I can spare you a quarter of an hour until the scones come out." Elspeth took a seat on one of the chairs surrounding the table and gestured to the detectives to do likewise. She folded her hands in her lap and regarded the inspector calmly.

"A few basic facts to start with," began Constable. "Am I right in thinking that you have been employed here for some while?"

"Indeed I have," replied Elspeth. "I've worked for Sir Richard and Lady Olivia for over twenty-five years."

"And is there a Mr. Carruthers?"

"Oh, bless you, no," smiled Elspeth. "Don't be fooled. 'Mrs' is just the courtesy title they always used to give to the housekeeper in the old days, whether she was married or not. And of course, Sir Richard was very much a traditionalist, just like his father, and with Lady Olivia having been brought up in a big house, they very much keep to the old ways. So no, I'm not married. I never have been. I'm happily wedded to the job." There was an aura of contentment about her that tended to confirm her words.

"Have you been the housekeeper all that time?"

"No. I used to be the assistant to the previous housekeeper, Mrs. Ford, but then I took over the post when she retired about fifteen years ago."

"And other than Mr. Pelham, are you the only member of staff in the house?"

"That's correct, inspector."

"Isn't that rather arduous for one lady on her own?" Constable delicately left the matter of age out of the enquiry.

"Oh, it's a very easy house to look after really," declared Elspeth stoutly. "What with only Sir Richard and her ladyship in residence. And Master James from time to time, of course." A barely perceptible sniff. "But I do have Mrs. Jenkins who comes up from the village every morning to do the rough work – the dusting and the vacuuming and making the beds and so on – but she's usually gone by eleven o'clock."

"So your responsibilities would be ...?"

"I look after the valuable items," said Elspeth with a touch of pride. "Lady Olivia has some lovely pieces of porcelain. Quite valuable too. Her grandfather left several of them to her, and he was a

169

great connoisseur, they say, so of course they do require an especially delicate touch. And of course, there's also Sir Richard's oriental collection in the cabinet in the library."

"Yes, we have seen that, Mrs. Carruthers. In fact, it was one of the things we were particularly interested in ..."

"Oh, I know what you're going to say," interrupted Elspeth. "That horrible dagger. Mr. Pelham told me all about it. He said, when he found Sir Richard, there it was, sticking right out of him." She gave a shudder of horror. "It's so sharp. Once or twice I've nearly cut myself just picking it up to dust. I always did think that cabinet should have been kept locked with that inside it."

"You're probably right. We believe it possible that whoever was responsible for using it to attack Sir Richard may simply have seized it on the spur of the moment."

Elspeth shook her head in puzzlement. "No, that can't be, inspector," she declared firmly.

Constable senses were alerted. "Why do you say that, Mrs. Carruthers?"

"Of course, it normally lives in there for anyone to see, and quite often, if guests came to the house, Sir Richard would show them his collection, especially if he had a new piece that he'd just added. But on that particular morning, when I went in to do the library at about a quarter past eleven, the dagger wasn't there. And I remember it was that day, because I don't do the inside of the cabinet every day on account of it being closed to keep out the dust most of the time, but this was my day to do the inside. And the dagger was gone then – I'm certain of it."

Constable pondered for a moment, and glanced across to check that Copper was noting all the relevant details. "Hmmm. We shall look into that, Mrs. Carruthers. But for the moment I'd like to move on. Can you tell me when would have been the last time you saw Sir Richard?"

"That would have been just after lunch, inspector. He came into the kitchen to apologise to me for Mr. James not having been there. You see," Elspeth explained, "when Sir Richard and her ladyship were alone in the house, they would normally just have a light luncheon, very often something cold, but when Master James comes to stay, Lady Olivia usually likes me to do a little extra something. And it so happens that I'd made a soufflé, but Master James didn't appear, and she and Sir Richard found it all a little embarrassing. That's why he made a point of coming to see me afterwards. He was always such a gentleman. He always hated it when any of the staff were put out."

"And you didn't see him after that?" Constable sought to confirm.

"No, inspector. I was busy in here for most of the afternoon, because the family were entertaining in the evening. Her ladyship popped in to let me know that there would be an extra dinner guest, so I was preparing the food as soon as I came back downstairs after my afternoon nap. I always try to take a little nap after lunch," she confided. "After all, I'm not getting any younger, and her ladyship is always very understanding."

"I'm sure," smiled Constable. "Which would then bring us on to the evening."

"I did spend a little time out in the rest of the house on and off," said Elspeth. "Of course, I was mainly in here making sure that all the dinner preparations were in hand, but I was in the drawing room at about a quarter to eight when Lady Olivia came in. I try to be finished in there before the family appear, but it's not always easy to gauge, because Mr. Pelham doesn't sound a gong."

"And you were in the drawing room because ...?"

"I always like to check the flowers and make sure the drinks are all topped up. And it's just as well I did, because the whisky decanter was almost empty, so I'd just refilled it and fetched a fresh jug of water and some ice when her ladyship came in."

"And do you prepare the drinks for the family?"

"Oh no." Elspeth looked slightly shocked. "That wouldn't be my job at all. That would be Mr. Pelham's province, except that the family always saw to their own drinks before dinner. Sir Richard preferred it that way, because he was always one for his whisky and water, and he was most particular about the proportions. They had to be just right. And if anyone ever mentioned the question of ice, he would give them such a glare!" A small smile. "As a good Scotswoman, I have to say I agreed with him."

"And the others?"

"Her ladyship? She usually has either a dry sherry or a gin and tonic. I remember she went to the table and poured herself a gin as soon as she arrived. The ice is for her."

"Not whisky?"

"Oh no. She always says she doesn't like the smell. And then there's Master James. He always drinks Sir Richard's best whisky – well, he would."

"So the family were all gathered together by the time you left the room?"

"Sir Richard came in while I was there. And I saw Master James coming downstairs just as I was leaving the drawing room. I assumed that was where he was going. But I didn't see because I'd gone back through the door to the kitchen by then."

"Did you happen to see any more of the family or their guests at any other point?" enquired Constable.

Elspeth thought for a moment. "I did," she stated. "I remember, I had just gone to put the centrepiece of flowers on the dining table at about twenty past eight, and I was going back towards the kitchen when I saw her ladyship going upstairs. And I remember thinking at the time, seeing the expression on her face, she looked as if she was upset over something, and in fact, she still had the handkerchief in her hand from earlier, so for all I know, she could have been wiping away a tear, if that doesn't sound too melodramatic. But then I was away back to the kitchen, and what with everything that went on afterwards, I didn't give it another thought."

"Did you by any chance see where she'd come from?"

A frown. "No, I don't think so, inspector. She was already on the staircase when I saw her. I assume she must have come from the drawing room. That's where I'd last seen her."

"And as you say, the events we're looking into occurred immediately after that."

"That's so, sir. Just when I got back to the kitchen, I thought I heard what might have been a car out at the back, and I remember wondering if perhaps Master James and Lady Olivia had had some sort of an argument, and he'd gone off with a flea in his ear, but of course, that wasn't so. And then there came the bang, which they said afterwards was the gunshot. I came out into the hall, and Mr. Pelham was just going into the library, when all of the sudden there was a loud banging at the front door, and I thought 'Well, Mr. Pelham can't be in two places at once', so I went to open the door and let young Mr. Elliott in. And at the same time, her ladyship and Master James appeared, as well as that Mrs. Baverstock out of the drawing room. And then straight after that, Mr. Pelham came out of the library and broke the news to us that Sir Richard had been killed, and then he telephoned the police." Elspeth stopped to catch her breath after this dramatic recital.

As if to place a punctuation mark at the end of Elspeth's evidence, the kitchen timer began to ring.

"Your baking would appear to be ready, Mrs. Carruthers," remarked Constable with a smile, as the housekeeper rose to remove the tray from the oven. "And very fine they look," he added, surveying the golden-topped scones.

"All in the timing, inspector," replied Elspeth.

"I imagine it's a great deal easier with a modern oven, rather than the old range your predecessors had to use."

"It is that," she agreed. "People say those were the days, but they really weren't. All that nasty dirty coal, making such a mess. That's one of the reasons this house is so easy to keep clean. Not a lump of coal in the place."

"But ..." Constable was puzzled. "But the fire in the library ..."

Elspeth chuckled. "Oh, bless you, inspector, that's not a real fire. I'm surprised you didn't notice. No, there aren't any real fires in the house at all. About five years ago, Sir Richard had all the fireplaces in the house converted to gas with those things that look like coal or logs. He might have been a traditionalist in many ways, but he wasn't averse to a bit of modernity when it suited him, and they save so much time and mess."

"Gas ..." mused Constable.

"That's right," continued Elspeth. "He had the house connected to the village's mains supply at the same time. It cost a pretty penny, I think, but I'm sure it's been a saving in the long run."

"And before that?"

"Oh, the house had gas before then, but that was from its own gas plant. I think they thought they were very modern when the house was built. There's a great big ugly piece of machinery out in one of the buildings around the stable yard, but the place has been disused and locked up for years. No, everything's natural gas from the mains now."

175

Chapter 12

"Questions, questions, questions," muttered Andy Constable in an undertone. The two detectives stood at the foot of the dimly-lit stairwell of Effingham Hall.

"Sorry, guv?"

The inspector came back to himself. "I was just thinking, sergeant," he said. "It seems to me that the more questions I ask, the more questions pop up to join them."

"Isn't that usually the way it is, guv?" replied Dave Copper. "And then you keep on asking questions, and then eventually the answers start fitting into place, and all of a sudden, you've got your jigsaw."

Constable smiled. "I think I detect the notorious Copper power of positive thinking coming into play, if I'm not much mistaken."

"That's what I'm here for, guv," grinned Copper. "And if you need any help, I've got my notebook here, full of goodies, which you are very welcome to take a look through."

Constable recoiled in mock horror. "Thank you for the very kind offer, sergeant, but I've got quite enough things swirling round in my brain already without adding to the stock of them just at the moment. In due course, yes, I will trawl through what you've got, although I suspect that I will end up with severe eye strain and a blinding headache from trying to decipher your scrawl."

"Decent calligraphy takes time, sir," retorted Copper, a touch huffily. "That's a luxury you don't usually allow me."

"True. And don't think your efforts go unappreciated."

"Well, thanks for that, guv," said Copper, mollified. "So, what next?"

"Or where, or who?"

"Are we back to Kipling's '*six honest serving men*', guv?"

"I think we are. And well remembered, by the way. We'll make a scholar of you yet."

"Can I suggest, sir, as we're here, that here might be a good place to start. That is, if you've got any more of those questions of yours for the people in the house."

"I certainly have. Lady Olivia, for a start. I think, when we first spoke to her, she was evasive, to say the least, about Sir Richard's relationship with her and these other women of his. I think there's more to find out there. So all we need to do is see if the lady is available."

"You'll want Mr. Pelham, sir. I don't think he'd approve if we were just to go barging round the place looking for her."

"Very true. So where, I wonder, is a butler to be found at this hour of the day?"

"May I help you, sir?" The voice at Constable's elbow almost caused him to jump out of his skin, as Pelham materialised alongside him. "I'm sorry, sir. I didn't mean to startle you. I've just been attending to something in the dining room, and as I came out I thought I heard my name."

"You move very quietly, Mr. Pelham," commented Constable, recovering himself.

177

"It is the training, sir," said Pelham complacently. "What was it you were wanting?"

"To have a word with Lady Olivia, if that's possible."

"Her ladyship is in the morning room, sir. If you will follow me, I will see if she will receive you."

"How very grand," murmured Copper to Constable, as the butler disappeared into the morning room. A low exchange of voices could be heard.

"Would you please come this way, inspector." Pelham held back the door to allow the two detectives to enter the room.

Lady Olivia rose from her seat at a small and exquisite Boule writing-desk in the window of the room, leaving a scatter of black-edged cards on its surface. "Good day, inspector."

"I hope we're not disturbing you, your ladyship."

"No more than you must, I suppose." A faint smile. "And you take me away from a task which I do not particularly relish. I've received notification that I may arrange Richard's funeral, and so I was in the process of doing so. Not that it will be a particularly large affair. There is, after all, next to no family. And the last thing I want is the whole world watching. So we shall have a brief service for a few people in the village church – that's where the Effingham family vault is."

"When is it to be?"

"The day after tomorrow."

"I hope you'll allow me to attend." An inclination of the head was Lady Olivia's only response. "But now, and I apologise for any insensitivity in the timing, I would be glad if I could ask a few questions."

"We all have our duty to do, inspector," said Lady Olivia. "Shall we sit down?" She moved to a sofa in front of the fireplace as the police officers took a seat opposite. "What would you like to know?"

Constable drew a breath. "When we spoke before, Lady Olivia, you mentioned that the last time you saw your husband was in the drawing room before dinner. He left the room to attend to a visitor, and you told us that you left the room yourself some minutes later. Now, one of the members of your staff happened to see you, and noticed that you seemed to be upset. I wondered if that might be relevant."

All expression left Lady Olivia's face. "How very observant people can be, Mr. Constable." She sounded determined to give nothing away.

The inspector persisted. "I know this may be sensitive territory, your ladyship, but in a case of this kind, I'm afraid that personal sensitivities count for very little. I have to ask you, is what we've been told true?"

Lady Olivia sighed. "Oh, very well, inspector. Yes, I was upset over something Richard had said."

"While you were together in the drawing room?"

"No. Earlier."

"That would seem to be a somewhat delayed reaction. I was wondering if it might have had to do with the arrival of Sir Richard's visitor. I mean, the unexpected one. The lady."

179

Lady Olivia drew herself up with dignity. "It's obvious, inspector, that there's no point in shilly-shallying. You've evidently been told a great deal more about the situation concerning my husband than I hoped would ever emerge. A woman has her pride, Mr. Constable. And I'm not a fool. I'm perfectly well aware that Richard has never been a saint. Not even when we were first married, although I did my best to overlook the fact in the hope that the matter would remedy itself. But he has always had ... women friends."

"And you had reason to believe that your husband's visitor was one of these? Were you aware of who it was?"

"It was fairly obvious, inspector. Pelham was clearly being painfully discreet when he came to tell Richard about the caller, and Richard had that expression on his face – it's one a wife learns to interpret quite quickly, inspector. But as James was in the room, I chose to say nothing. And then Julia Baverstock arrived a few minutes later, so James poured her a drink."

"Can I ask what?" interrupted Constable.

"Oh. A sherry, I think. Yes, it was, because I remember he fumbled with the decanter as he was putting it back and spilt some on his trousers, so he needed to go and change them, leaving me to sit making excuses to Julia as to why Richard wasn't there."

"And after that?"

"It got steadily more awkward, inspector. Julia was rather tight-lipped, and in the end I felt I just couldn't sit there making conversation any longer – not with that Wadsworth woman in the house - so I told Julia that I was feeling a little faint and wanted to go upstairs to wash my face before dinner. Feeble, I know, but it was the best I could think of. And that's all I can tell you, inspector. If I was seen going upstairs, surely you should be satisfied that that is where I was at the time of the shot." Lady Olivia gave the inspector a challenging look. "Which I assume is the purpose of this questioning. You evidently seem to have some idea that I was linked with my husband's death in some way."

"I'm sure I've said nothing to give you that impression, your ladyship," returned Constable mildly. "And we need to look into all aspects of the case if we are to find out who killed your husband."

"Even if it means washing the family's private dirty linen in public, inspector?" challenged Lady Olivia. "Well, I suppose you have your duty to do."

"As you yourself pointed out, Lady Olivia."

A snort. "Well, if you have nothing further to ask me, I have matters to attend to." Lady Olivia rose and pushed a bell at the side of the fireplace. "Pelham will show you out." Without a backward glance, she resumed her seat at her desk as the door to the hall opened.

"Mr. Pelham." Constable forestalled the butler as he led the way across the hall towards the front door. "I wonder if Mr. Booker-Gresham is around. We'd like a word."

Pelham turned. "I'm afraid not, sir. Master James has gone up to London this morning."

"Oh?"

181

"Yes, sir. He mentioned having to attend a meeting at his firm's offices in the City. It was apparently a matter of some urgency. I understand he intends to return later today."

"Ah. Well, perhaps we'll be able to catch him then. If you see him, would you tell him that we'd like to speak to him?"

"I shall pass on the message, sir," replied Pelham gravely. "Good morning." He held the door open, and the detectives found themselves on the front steps of Effingham Hall almost before they were aware of it.

*

"I can't remember being put in my place twice in such a short time, guv," remarked Dave Copper with a wry grin. "And Lady Olivia seemed such a nice woman when I first met her."

"Ah," said Andy Constable, "but that was on a case when you were working in the family's interests. Perhaps she sees it differently this time."

There seemed to be something nagging at Copper's mind. "Guv ..."

"What?"

"I've got that itch."

"I'm hoping you're going to tell me it's that one at the back of your brain."

"It is, sir. You know you're always going on about inconsistencies ... and I'm sure I could look it up in my notes if you wanted me to ..."

"Don't drivel, man. Out with it."

"It's something Lady Olivia said about when she went upstairs, sir. Well, two things, really. When we came here first, she told you she was upstairs at the time of the gunshot because she'd gone up because she wanted to get a handkerchief. But Mrs. Carruthers has just told us that when she saw Lady Olivia going upstairs, she had a handkerchief in her hand. And now her ladyship says she went up to wash her face. They can't all be true ... can they?"

"I suppose it's possible," mused Constable slowly. "Perhaps she used the handkerchief so then needed to get a fresh one, and the 'washing the face' business was just an excuse to get out of the room, which is what she told us. But you're right. It doesn't absolutely hang together."

"And Mrs. Carruthers did say that the lady looked upset."

"You're right. And well spotted," said Constable approvingly. "We'll let those thoughts bubble under quietly. But there are plenty of other people to talk to, so there's no sense in rushing our fences and jumping to conclusions."

"Can I make a suggestion, sir?"

"Go ahead."

"Why don't we do what we did the first time we came here, and retrace our steps round the circuit of people? I could drive, and then you can sit and think profound thoughts, like you do."

"You just want another chance to drive a decent car instead of that haven of superannuated coffee cups and crisp packets that you drive," smiled Constable. "But yes, it's not at all a bad idea. As long as you remember where we're going. Don't expect me to fiddle with that phone of yours for directions."

"I happen to have extremely good route recall, guv," replied Copper with dignity. "So, if you're happy, we'll be on our way to visit Mrs. Baverstock."

"Good. She's another lady who wasn't entirely candid about the events of the day of the murder when we went to see her first. In the light of what Mr. Diggory said, evasive, to say the least. So let's find what holes we can pick in her story."

"Inspector!" There was a note of surprise in Julia Baverstock's voice as she opened the door to the two police officers. "I didn't expect to see you again so soon."

"We happened to be in the vicinity," lied Constable smoothly, " and I thought we might take the opportunity to resolve one or two queries that have arisen since we first talked. I hope it isn't inconvenient, our calling on you unannounced."

"No, not at all." Julia nevertheless sounded slightly disconcerted. "Do come through." She led the way to the room where she had first spoken to the detectives.

Constable decided to come straight to the point. "Mrs. Baverstock, you indicated to us that your conversations with Sir Richard on the day of his death were entirely amicable. That wasn't true, was it?"

Julia seemed taken aback by the directness of the question. "I like to think we were both perfectly civilised ..." she blustered.

"Nonsense!" broke in Constable brusquely. "Please don't waste your time and ours by trying to avoid the truth, Mrs. Baverstock. There was a witness to the scene which took place between yourself and Sir Richard, and they have described it as anything but amicable. You were making accusations regarding his stable's handling of your highly valuable racehorse, and according to our witness, you left the premises in a state of considerable anger."

"Oh, what if I did?" responded Julia defiantly. "And you'd have done the same if you'd been in my place. I'd lost a very valuable asset through no fault of my own, and I wanted the matter resolved. But it was obvious that we were going to get nowhere – Richard was fobbing me off with promises that he was going to look into matters – so I left."

"Agreeing to return later for dinner."

"Yes. I refused to let matters lie, and I hoped that perhaps Olivia might have some sort of softening effect on Richard's attitude."

"So you went back to Effingham Hall in the evening?"

"Yes."

"But Sir Richard wasn't there in the room when you arrived?"

"No. I think I've told you all this already, inspector," said Julia impatiently.

"Merely seeking to ensure that we have all the details correct, madam," said Constable smoothly. "So, you were in the drawing room with the other members of the family ..."

"For a while, yes. And then that idiot James spilt the sherry, so then he went to change, and not long after that, Olivia went off somewhere. To be frank, I was glad she did – you could see her mind wasn't on the conversation."

"So then you were left alone. And there was

still no sign of Sir Richard. So, in fact, you're confirming that you didn't see him at all that evening?"

There was a very long pause. "Oh, all right, inspector," flashed Julia. "Yes, if you must know, I did."

"Perhaps you'd like to tell us about it, Mrs. Baverstock," invited Constable softly.

Julia took a deep breath to steady herself. "I admit it. I was still seething from that afternoon, and somebody had said that Richard was in the library, so after Olivia left, I went in there to give Richard a piece of my mind."

"And how did he respond?"

"He didn't, inspector. He just sat there looking at me with that stupid contemptuous look on his face. He had a habit of doing that whenever somebody was saying something to him that he didn't want to hear."

"But you let him know in no uncertain terms what your feelings were?"

"Yes, I did. And I have to say that it felt so good to get the whole thing off my chest. When I'd finished, I turned on my heel and walked out on him. To be frank, I don't know why I didn't just keep walking, out of his house and out of his life. But for some reason, I didn't. I just went back to the drawing room and sat there on my own waiting for dinner." She snorted. "Not that I was looking forward to it much."

"Leaving the matter of your dispute over your racehorse still unresolved," said Constable. "Which is the way it will presumably have to remain."

"Not if I've got anything to do with it,"
declared Julia firmly. "I can make a claim against the
business. Not, if the whispers I hear are true, that I
may have much luck there. But if all else fails, I can
pursue the estate. I'm not letting this go, inspector."

*

"Secrets and lies, guv," said Copper, as the
two detectives climbed back into the car. "And she's
a lady with a temper, you can't deny that. So surely
that puts her well back into the frame. She was on
the spot, and she had plenty of reasons to have it in
for Sir Richard."

"But to kill him?" responded Constable. "With
all this horse business still hanging in the air? Would
that have been in her own self-interest?"

"People lose logic in the heat of the moment,
sir."

"True. But she has one thing in her favour.
Immediately after the shot was fired, she appeared
in the doorway of the drawing room. Unless she's
mastered the art of teleportation, she's someone
else who can't be in two places at once."

"And since we can't either, guv," grinned
Copper, "I suppose I'd better get on with driving us
to our next port of call."

"Which I take to be the Effingham stables."

"Do you want me to give them a call to check
that Mr. Worcester is on the premises, sir? We don't
want a wasted journey."

"I think not," said Constable. "Why give the
gentleman warning? It seems to me that the element
of surprise is far more efficacious in producing

187

unguarded revelations."

Simon Worcester was just about to get into his car as the detectives arrived at the offices of the Effingham racing establishment. "Will this take long, inspector? I have to ... I was just about to go out."

"We'll try not to keep you, Mr. Worcester," said Constable with a bland but implacable smile, "but I was hoping to straighten out a few things. Would we be more comfortable inside?"

Seated once again in Simon's office, Constable indicated to Copper to produce his notebook and prepare to make notes. Simon, observing this, uneasily brought out a whisky bottle from his desk drawer and poured himself a shaky drink.

"On the afternoon of Sir Richard's death," began the inspector, "you visited him at home. You told us that you needed to deal with some routine paperwork. It sounds to me as if you were very punctilious when it came to keeping your documentation in order."

"Yes," said Simon hesitantly. "You need to be."

"Except, perhaps, when it came to the insurance on 'Last Edition'," pounced Constable.

"I ... I don't know what you're getting at, inspector."

"Please, Mr. Worcester," sighed Constable. "There was a conversation heard, and if you absolutely insist I can have Sergeant Copper here recite the salient points, which informed us that there was a dispute between Sir Richard and Mrs. Julia Baverstock over the fate of her racehorse. And the question of the horse's insured status was at the heart of this. Or should I say, non-insured status."

Simon looked evasive. "If it hadn't been for that damned horse of Julia's, everything would have been fine."

"So there were problems. Which, I take it, would leave the business liable to pay any compensation. How very fortunate, then, that the business is in such a good financial position under your stewardship." The wolfish smile appeared again. "I assume that's the case, anyway. Although ..." Constable turned to his junior. "Copper, remind me. Didn't someone mention something about whispers concerning the financial health of the stables?"

Copper caught on swiftly. "I believe they did, sir."

"And ..." Constable suddenly recalled a snippet of conversation, and took a guess. "Wasn't there some hint of gambling losses?"

Simon crumpled. "Rumours. It's all just rumours. And people taking their horses away from us and putting them with other trainers because of some poisonous gossip. It would all have sorted itself out. And I might have borrowed some money from the business, and some of the bills hadn't been paid on time, including that insurance, but really, it was all Richard's fault."

Constable regarded Simon disbelievingly. "You're saying that your old school friend, the man who placed you in charge of the financial organisation of this business, is responsible for the mishandling of its money?"

"Richard should have checked the insurances," insisted Simon. "They were all in his name, not mine. And I told him when I went to see him that afternoon that everything would be put right, and that's why I phoned up that evening."

"To reassure him?"

"Yes." Simon's face was growing shinier.

"You called from here?"

"Yes. Well, here, or up at the stables themselves. I really can't remember exactly."

"But either here on the land-line, or from the stables on your mobile?"

"Yes. I just use whichever phone is handiest. Does it matter? The point was, when I called, it was just after Richard had been shot, so I drove straight over there to see what I could do. But you know all that. I got there when the other police car did. They'll tell you."

"That can certainly be confirmed, sir." Constable got to his feet. "Well, I don't think we need to trouble you any further at this juncture, Mr. Worcester. Obviously, in the light of what you've told us, we have various matters that we'll want to look into further. But for now, we'll be out of your way." As the detectives left the office, Simon was pouring a further large measure of whisky.

Chapter 13

"Pull in here."

"Righty-ho, guv." Dave Copper obediently pulled the car into a lay-by.

"Something's bugging you, sergeant," said Andy Constable. "I can hear the wheels churning. Out with it."

"It's what Simon Worcester said about borrowing money from the business. I thought to myself, 'Hello, here's a nice motive'. But you let it pass without saying anything."

"Just because I didn't comment at the time, sergeant, doesn't mean that it didn't register with me," replied Constable. "Of course it did. But we don't know the scale of the borrowing. It might only have been minor amounts. We don't why it happened. For all we know, Mr. Worcester has some sort of illicit gambling habit that has led to losses which he's had to cover by dipping into the till. That bears checking out. We don't know if it contributed to the alleged shakiness of the company's finances, or whether those are exacerbated by the threatened dispute over 'Last Edition'. But don't think for a moment that I'm not bearing all these possibilities in mind."

"Oh. Right. Sorry, guv," said Copper humbly. "And there's another thing, of course. Even if he had a motive, there's still the problem of opportunity. He was in the house earlier, he was in the house later, but he was never there at the right time."

"So many things to consider," smiled Constable with a sideways look at his junior

191

colleague. "And we shall. But for the moment, rather than perusing the stock of information we have, I think we should see if we can add to it."

"And that's my cue to drive on, I reckon, guv."

"Well spotted. On round to Knaggs End, and we'll pay another call on Mrs. Wadsworth."

The car's wheels crunched on the gravel of the drive as the detectives pulled into Hilton House alongside Sarah Wadsworth's sports model.

"Well, it looks as if she's home," said Copper. "Are you sure you're up to this, guv," he enquired warily. "You and the lady didn't quite hit it off last time we were here."

"Oh, I think I'm rather better prepared for Mrs. Wadsworth this time," said Constable. "We know somewhat more than we did before. And I'm particularly interested in hearing what she's got to say about the will."

Seated in the garden room overlooking the lawns at the back of the house, Sarah regarded the detectives with barely concealed hostility. She drew a cigarette from her gold case and lit it from an adjacent onyx table lighter. There was no attempt to offer refreshments. "Well?" She sat back and blew a stream of smoke.

'It's like that, is it?' thought Constable. 'Kid gloves off, then.' "Tell me, Mrs. Wadsworth, exactly how conversant were you with the provisions of Sir Richard Effingham's will?"

Sarah looked momentarily disconcerted, but recovered herself swiftly. Her lips smiled, but no warmth reached her eyes. "That stupid man thought money was the answer to everything," she retorted waspishly. "As if a hundred thousand pounds would pay for everything I've given him over fifteen years."

Constable was startled by her sudden vehemence. "You make it sound, Mrs. Wadsworth, as if your relationship with Sir Richard was based on financial considerations. And forgive me, but some people might say that there is a word for that."

"Oh, don't be so middle-class and ridiculous, inspector," snapped Sarah. She seemed to realise the impression she was creating, and softened slightly. "There was nothing of the ... let's be refined and call it 'kept woman' ... about our relationship. When it started out, he did genuinely sweep me off my feet. He was a very glamorous man then, and I was very fond of him in those days. Yes ... in fact, you could probably say I loved him. And even when I got to know his nature in time, I could even overlook his little ... excursions." She gave a soft and bitter laugh. "I dare say I never knew the half of it. I shouldn't be surprised if he'd gone around scattering by-blows all over the county. Probably more than one. But I'm not like that damned wife of his, prepared to put up with anything."

"No?" encouraged the inspector, unwilling to disrupt the flow.

"Not when it started to become blatant. I knew perfectly well he had another woman. And at his age, that sort of thing starts to look absurd."

"So you elected to have it out with him face to face and end it all. And you decided to visit him at his house."

"Yes. Look, Mr. Constable, I've already told you all this."

"Yes, Mrs. Wadsworth," countered Constable, "But you neglected to mention the will when we talked before. I should have thought you might have done so. Unless, of course, it slipped your mind. In the heat of the conversation."

"Of course not. I told Richard how things stood. He showed me the will, and I just told him I didn't want his wretched money. He didn't seem to care, which I am prepared to admit made me seethe even more." A pause as if recollecting the moment. "So I set fire to the damned will and walked out."

"Leaving the way you came? Through the house?"

"No, I did not, inspector. I had no intention of being looked down on by Pelham, who for all I know was lurking outside the door listening to everything that went on. So I went out of the french windows. Why? What does it matter? You know I left, and you know what time I got back here, so if you are trying to place me in the house when Richard was shot, you are wasting your time."

Constable leaned forward. "That's an extremely smart cigarette case you have there, Mrs. Wadsworth," he remarked out of the blue. "Might I take a closer look at it?"

"What?" Sarah seemed utterly bewildered at the abrupt change of tack. "Yes, if you wish." She handed it across.

Constable examined it. "That's a very elegant design. Was it a gift, may I ask?"

"Yes, as it happens, it was." Sarah continued to look puzzled.

To Copper's surprise, Constable did not

pursue the matter, and suddenly stood. "I think that's all I need to know for the moment, Mrs. Wadsworth. But I expect we'll be speaking again in due course." Copper thought he caught a hint of a threat in the inspector's words. "No sign of Mr. Wadsworth, I take it," remarked Constable as he headed for the front door. "I wonder if I'll ever get to meet him. Perhaps at Sir Richard's funeral the day after tomorrow."

"I think it unlikely, Mr. Constable," retorted Sarah icily. "My husband is on the way to Tokyo. He won't be back for a fortnight."

"So you will have to grieve alone," said Constable lightly. He turned and descended the front steps, Copper in his wake.

*

"So what was all that about, guv?" enquired the puzzled sergeant, as the two detectives seated themselves once more in the saloon bar of the Four Horseshoes, Dave Copper having accepted with alacrity his superior's suggestion of a break for lunch.

"What in particular?" queried Andy Constable. "The will? The husband? The funeral?"

"The cigarette case. Okay, so it was a present. We can put two and two together and guess that it was a gift from Sir Richard, but that's hardly surprising, is it? Isn't that the sort of thing the rich man might well give to the kept woman, to use Mrs. Wadsworth's own words?"

"Of course it is, sergeant. But you're being unusually slow on the uptake, if I may say so. She's told us everything we need to know about a couple of the items that were found at the scene of the murder. She said she set fire to the will. Fine. Now we know who did that. And she set fire to it with ...?"

"Of course! Sorry, guv. Being a bit thick. With the matching cigarette lighter, which she either dropped by accident or chucked down as another gesture of rejection. And then, as she said, she walked out."

"Hmmm. I wonder if that's all she did."

"Is that another one for your quiet moments of reflection, guv?" grinned Copper.

"You know me too well," said Constable with an answering smile. "But for now, we shall turn from that and instead take another look at the bar menu of this excellent hostelry. Where," he added, "we shall be in danger of becoming regulars if we can't resolve this case before too long."

Copper perused the list of fare. "'Local specialities', they reckon, guv," he remarked. "So what on earth is Old Spot Stroganoff when it's at home?" he asked. "Doesn't sound too local to me."

"And that is because you are pure townie," responded Constable. "Never heard of Gloucester Old Spot pigs? As tasty a piece of pork as you'll find, although I'll grant you, more Mercia than Wessex, but let's not be picky. And Stroganoff is originally Russian, so also not strictly local, but with a bit of luck the other ingredients are. Onions, mushrooms, a slosh of cream – sounds good to me."

"I think I'll settle for the mutton hotpot," said Copper. "It looks a bit more down-to-earth, suitable for those of us in the lower ranks. I'm happy to watch you enjoy your exotic foreign food from a safe distance. What was it somebody said about 'lying in the gutter but looking at the stars'?"

Constable smilingly shook his head in amazement. "Sergeant, you never cease to amaze me. I never had you down as a fan of Oscar Wilde. However, as this is probably neither the time nor the place for a philosophical discussion, I suggest you take yourself up to the bar and place the order. And don't forget to get a receipt."

As the two detectives finished their meal, Copper became aware that his superior had fallen silent. "Something on your mind, guv? You're doing that 'quiet moment of reflection' thing, and you usually get me out of the way before you start on that."

The inspector smiled faintly. "Sorry about that. No, I was just musing over something Mrs. Wadsworth let drop during one of her little rants. It slipped past me at the time, but now I'm thinking it's time to go and put one and one together to make three." He put down his cutlery, drained the last few drops of shandy in his glass, and stood. "Come on – let's go and pay Owen Elliott a visit." He headed towards the door, a somewhat bemused-looking Dave Copper in his wake.

When he answered the door of his flat, Owen Elliott looked if anything even more morose and dishevelled than on the detectives' first visit. Registering the identity of his callers with dull eyes, he stood back wordlessly to allow them to enter and then climbed the stairs wearily to his sitting room, where he slumped into his previous position on the sagging beanbag.

The police officers exchanged mute glances as they sat uninvited on the sofa. "Mr. Elliott," began Constable, "we've been learning rather more about the late Sir Richard Effingham since we last came to see you."

"Yeah," replied Owen, "looks like we all learned quite a lot about him."

The inspector was not to be deflected. "You told us about your recent run-in with Sir Richard. What you didn't tell us about was all the background. We've had to hear about that from an entirely different source. About how you were always to be found around the horses up at Sir Richard's house. How he virtually took you under his wing. He had you apprenticed as a jockey. You were, in effect, his protégé. More, in fact, than just an ordinary local boy from the village with a love of horses."

"So?" Owen's face wore a mixture of wariness and defiance.

"One of the things we have come to realise about Sir Richard," continued Constable calmly, "was that he had a considerable fondness for female companionship. We've spoken to someone who described him as very glamorous when he was younger. And that same person threw up the possibility that, although Sir Richard and Lady Olivia had no children of their own, there might be other … offspring. Outside the family. Would you have any thoughts on that?"

After the heavy silence which descended on the room for several long moments, Owen suddenly became animated. He sprang to his feet and began to pace. "How could he do it to me?" he cried in anguish, as Copper looked on in amazement. "My own father!"

"You knew?" asked Constable softly.

"Yes," said Owen. "My mother told me just before she died." He subsided as suddenly as he had begun. "I'd no idea. God, what an idiot I was. The squire's son and the village girl. Just like some trashy story." A bitter laugh. "I'm surprised he didn't put it into one of his own books. My mother made me promise I'd never say a word. Swore me to secrecy. I think she was ashamed, although these days, who cares? But then I knew why he'd taken an interest and arranged for me to be apprenticed and everything, and then taken me on to ride for his own stable. I was his own little private secret. The son he couldn't have. He must have felt so good about himself."

"And until recently, nothing happened to mar that relationship. I mean, between employer and employee, naturally. I don't mean to imply anything else. But then, of course, came the incident with 'Last Edition'."

"That's right." Owen had calmed down considerably. "And I told him over and over again that the accident wasn't my fault, and there were other people to back me up, but it didn't make any difference. He said he'd trained me better than that. I said to him, 'How am I supposed to earn a living now?', but he refused to listen."

"And nevertheless, you went to see him again on the day of his death. With a view to having it out with him? Revealing what you knew?"

199

"Something like that. But I never got there in time, did I?"

"As you've told us, Mr. Elliott," said Constable. "And since you have a witness to the time you arrived at the front door, the facts seem all very clear from that point onwards." He stood. "I don't know if you've been informed, but Sir Richard's funeral is being arranged for the day after tomorrow. I imagine you'll wish to attend. I believe Sir Richard's will is likely to be read afterwards."

Owen seemed uncertain. Something indefinable flared in his eyes. "Maybe. I don't know."

"I think you probably should," said Constable. "Who knows – we may all learn more on that day." With that gnomic utterance, he turned and headed down the stairs, Copper following behind.

*

"That came out of nowhere," said Dave Copper in admiration. "How did you figure that out?"

"A bit of this, a bit of that," replied Andy Constable modestly. "It just kept nagging at me, just out of sight – why did Sir Richard act so generously towards Owen? Men in that position are probably more likely to be irritated by a young lad hanging about under their feet than to take an interest in his progress. And knowing what we know about Sir Richard's predilection for the ladies, there was obviously nothing untoward going on, so there had to be another reason. And when Mrs. Wadsworth made that remark about Sir Richard scattering by-blows around the place – and there's a nice old-fashioned expression, if you like – suddenly it all clicked. So I took a guess. Luckily, it paid off."

"Does it change our thinking, guv? I mean, it certainly accounts for the fact that Owen gets a mention in the will. And he does go on a lot about being on his uppers. It's another motive."

"Although we're still not certain that the will we've seen was the ultimate version, remember," countered Constable.

"But then we've still got the problem that Owen didn't come on the scene until after Sir Richard had been shot. So we've got no evidence that he knew about the will."

"But he did phone earlier. And I would give a great deal to know the contents of that conversation."

"Well, unless Mr. Pelham was very conveniently eavesdropping on the call, I can't see how you're going to get any further with that, guv," said Copper. "So what next?"

"As we're on the subject of beneficiaries of the will," said Constable, "there's still one we have to catch up with. So back to the car, I think, up to Effingham Hall, and we'll see if young Master James has returned from his wanderings."

The grey sports car which the detectives had previously seen parked in the stable yard now stood at the foot of the steps to the front door.

"Our Mr. Booker-Gresham has returned to the fold," remarked Constable, as he pulled in alongside. "Let's see if Mr. Pelham can winkle him out."

The detectives had only been waiting in the morning room for a matter of moments when the

201

door opened and James came hesitantly into the room. "Pelham said you wanted to see me, inspector."

"That's right, Mr. Booker-Gresham," said Constable heartily. "We've got one or two things to clear up. Shall we sit down?"

Taking a seat, James looked at the inspector nervously. "What is it you want, exactly? I've told you everything I know."

Constable chose not to reply directly. "You had an urgent meeting with your employers today, I think, sir. And you work in one of the financial houses in the City of London, don't you? I do hope it wasn't some sort of international financial crisis. Should we all be putting our savings into gold?" He raised his eyebrows and smiled affably.

James managed a feeble answering smile. "Oh, nothing at all like that, inspector."

"So, perhaps something more personal, was it? One doesn't like to pry ..." The inspector's voice hardened. "Unless it has a bearing on the murder I'm investigating. Does it?" James sat regarding Constable as a rabbit would a snake. "One of the items involved in that murder is, of course, a rather valuable oriental dagger which seems to have had a habit of appearing and disappearing in something of an unaccountable fashion. And here's a strange coincidence, Mr. Booker-Gresham. On the day of Sir Richard's death, you had left the house, and lo!, the dagger had gone missing from its usual place. You returned later, and so, mysteriously at some point, did the dagger. Not, then, in its usual place, but in a far more gruesome location – buried up to the hilt in the lifeless body of Sir Richard. All very melodramatic, sir. Now tell me, if you were a suspicious person, wouldn't you be inclined to conclude that there was a connection between these events?" Constable leaned back and waited.

James licked his lips. "Oh, you might as well know everything," he blurted. "It sounds as if you do anyway. Yes, it's true – I'm in a bit of a hole financially. I had some trades that went wrong. I wasn't doing anything dishonest – I just took the wrong side of a bet. It happens. The trouble was, I was dealing in sums I wasn't authorised to. So I tried to make it up before anyone found out, and I damn near got there. Just one or two more deals, and I'd have been home and dry, and nobody would have been any the wiser. But for some reason, I couldn't manage to get that last little distance. And I was getting steadily more desperate, because the longer it all went on, the more likely it was that somebody would realise what I'd been doing."

"So you resorted to drastic measures?"

"Yes," admitted James. "That's why I pinched the dagger. I know, I probably wasn't thinking very clearly, but I had an idea that it was worth a mint and I thought if I could turn it into cash, I could make things good and sort it all out afterwards. So I took it up to Christeby's in London that day to be valued for auction. Of course, I was being an idiot – they wouldn't touch it without proof of ownership or provenance or whatever it's called, and they sent me away with a dusty answer, so my only hope was to try to sneak it back where it came from before anyone noticed it was missing."

"And did you?" asked Constable.

"I couldn't," replied James simply. "I meant to as soon as I came back that afternoon, but Uncle Richard was there when I got to the house, and he went straight into the library, so I had to hide the dagger in the hall in the hope of putting it back later."

"And ...?"

"I never got the chance. There was always somebody about whenever I tried. Either Pelham was fiddling about in and out of the dining room, or Mrs. Carruthers was going around with flower arrangements. But I finally saw my chance in the evening, once people had gathered for dinner. Aunt Olivia was in the drawing room, and I knew Mrs. Carruthers and Pelham would be busy in the kitchen and the dining room, so I tried to sneak it back into the library then. Trouble was, the old man was in there, and he caught me with the dagger in my hand, realised what I was doing, and had a good go at me. I just chucked the dagger on his desk and ran for it, and went upstairs to my room." James was left slightly breathless at the end of his recital.

"You didn't leave the house?"

"No."

Constable paused for a moment. "Tell me, Mr. Booker-Gresham – I remember when we first spoke, the question of Sir Richard's will was mentioned. Were you familiar with the provisions of that will?"

"No," said James. "Why?"

"Because a will was present at the scene of your uncle's death. I wondered if you might have seen it. Particularly the clause in which he left you one hundred thousand pounds."

James looked astonished. "*How* much?" He closed his eyes for a moment, and then muttered 'Thank god' almost inaudibly.

"Indeed, sir. A substantial sum. Maybe enough to solve your immediate financial difficulties?" A nod from James. "And probably even more than you were hoping to realise from the sale of the dagger. The dagger which ended up in Sir Richard's body."

"But I've told you, that wasn't me. The dagger was lying on his desk when I last saw it. I didn't stick it into him, I swear it." A speculative gleam came into James' eyes. "Mind you," he said slowly, "for a hundred thousand pounds, I can see why you think I might have done."

*

"More motives than you can shake a stick at, guv," commented Copper, as the detectives descended the front steps of the Hall, leaving a rather shaken James Booker-Gresham in their wake. "The means too, whatever he says he did or did not do with the dagger. But you can't buck the fact that when that shot was fired, he was upstairs, so he couldn't have done it."

"I just wish we had that gun," said Constable. "It's one of the main pieces in the jigsaw, and I'm sure that wherever it is will tell us something crucial."

"It's bound to make an appearance sooner or later, guv," declared Copper stoutly.

As if in answer to his superior's prayer, a cry sounded from the corner of the house.

205

"Inspector Constable! Thank goodness you're here." Diggory came into view at a fast shamble, a long object festooned with dripping foliage in his hand. "Look what I've just found!" He came to a panting halt in front of the inspector, in his hand the unmistakeable shape of a shotgun.

"Copper, take charge of that, would you," ordered Constable briskly. "And since Mr. Diggory's prints are doubtless on it already, you'd better make sure we don't get any extraneous ones to muddy the waters."

"Ahead of you, guv," said Copper, producing a pair of thin latex gloves from a pocket before putting them on and carefully relieving the gardener of his burden.

"So, where was this, Mr. Diggory?" asked Constable.

"That was it, see, inspector," replied Diggory. "I didn't see it at first, on account of the muddy water." His agitation was clear.

"You'll have to be a little plainer than that, Mr. Diggory," said Constable patiently. "So calm down and take your time. What exactly happened?"

The gardener took a deep breath, blew out his cheeks, and seemed to gather his wits. "Her ladyship told me about the funeral, inspector. Said as how it is going to be the day after tomorrow, and I thought, if there's going to be people coming to the house, she'll want the place looking as spick and span as can be, so I'll make sure the garden's all up to scratch. Now everything's mostly all neat and tidy, but I remembered I still hadn't finished with the lily pond round on the west terrace. See, I'd made a start getting the weed out of it the day Sir Richard died ..."

"Yes, I remember you telling us you were working round there when you overheard the conversation between Sir Richard and Mrs. Baverstock."

"That's right, so I was." Diggory nodded his head sagely. "But after that, what with one thing and another, I never got around to making a proper job of it, so I thought I'd get it done now. And there I am, raking the rest of the weed out with the mud all stirred up, when all of a sudden my rake catches on something. I thought, 'Hello, what's this?', so I give it another tug, and blow me, up comes my gun. And I was just bringing it round to ask her ladyship what I ought to do, and there you were."

"Extremely fortunate timing, I agree," said Constable. "For which we probably have to thank Sergeant Copper's legendary power of positive thinking," he added, with a wry smile in the direction of his junior. "And this is definitely your weapon?"

"No doubt about it, inspector. I'd know it anywhere."

"Right, Mr. Diggory." The inspector became brisk again. "Leave this with us. Copper, we need to get this gun into the hands of SOCO immediately. There's some plastic wrap in the boot of my car. Let's get over there straight away." He unlocked the car and climbed in as Copper dealt with the shotgun, and moments later the car pulled away in a spurt of gravel, leaving a somewhat bemused gardener in its wake.

Chapter 14

"What, all day?" Andy Constable sounded irritated.

"Sorry, guv, but there's nothing I can do about it. Apparently they've pulled the case forward, and I have to give the crucial evidence for the prosecution. And then I'm going to have to hang around in case they need to call me back in."

"I thought you were looking unusually smart. Is that a new tie?"

"Present for my last birthday, guv," explained Dave Copper. "I've just never got around to wearing it before."

"Well, I suppose at least it's preferable to the one with robins and reindeer on it which girlfriend of yours gave you last Christmas. By the way, whatever happened there?"

"Long gone, sir."

"The tie or the girlfriend?"

"Both, guv. Not compatible with the job, unfortunately. Either of them." Copper did not sound too distressed. He checked his watch. "Look, sir, I really ought to get on. Sorry to leave you on your todd, but it's not as if you probably haven't got stuff to do."

"True."

"Sergeant Singleton said SOCO would get the results from the gun to you as soon as they could. She did ask after you yesterday. I told her you were waiting in the car."

"I thought I'd leave the field clear for you. As I thought there was a certain something going on when we visited her before, and since you're evidently unencumbered at the moment ..."

"No idea what you're talking about, guv," said Copper, clearing his throat in an embarrassed fashion and changing the subject rapidly. "Didn't the doctor promise to get his report to you today?"

"He did. I'm hoping for an email at some time this morning. Plus there are all sorts of considerations I need to turn over in my mind."

"Such as?"

"Things like wills, hip flasks, walking sticks. The rat poison. And mysterious cars which nobody drove. So if you can spare it, I'd like your notebook to pore over."

"No problem – all my notes on today's court case are in my old book." Copper handed over the notebook. "Why – are you planning to fit in some of your usual quiet thinking today, guv?" he enquired with an impish grin.

"If I ever get the chance to," growled Constable in mock reproof. "Go!"

"I've gone."

The sound of Copper's footsteps faded along the corridor, leaving the inspector in blissful silence. To a casual observer, he might have appeared to be dozing as he leaned back in his chair with eyes closed. They would have been very wrong.

It was almost an hour later, he was surprised to note on consulting his watch, that Constable was jolted out of his musings by the ping signifying the arrival of mail in his inbox. He checked the screen. The hoped-for report from Dr. Livermore. He clicked a few keys, and the printer in the corner of the office whirred into action. Collecting the pages, Constable settled himself back behind his desk to peruse the contents.

The report went into considerable detail, much of which Constable elected to skip over as either too abstruse and technical, or too gruesome. The meticulous analysis of the victim's stomach contents was one of the sections which the inspector decided to gloss over, satisfying himself with the not-unexpected conclusion that lunch had been Sir Richard's final meal, and a confirmation of the doctor's slightly surprising finding that the trainer had not ingested any of the poison which was found in the whisky glass. But it was not the factors which had not been the cause of Sir Richard's death that Constable was seeking. What occupied his attention was an explanation of the many things which could have been. How on earth, he had asked himself ever since viewing the body, did there come to be so many injuries?

A sudden thought struck him, and he picked up the phone. "Hello ... get me Technical ... D.I. Constable here. I'm looking over the evidence in the Effingham case ... that's right. Tell me, can you take a look at the file on the case, make a list of everyone we've spoken to, and get access to all their phone logs? ... yes, land-lines and mobiles, the lot ... from, let's say, nine o'clock on the morning of the murder to nine o'clock that evening. That'll cover the whole twelve hours up until our people arrived on the scene ... an hour? That long, eh?" A chuckle. "And if you could bring the results up to my office when you're done ... thanks." He replaced the phone and turned back to the paperwork in front of him.

The doctor's report dealt with the wounds to Sir Richard's body in the order in which he had shown them to the detectives at the murder scene. The language was long-winded and technical – the conclusions gave Constable considerable food for thought. Attention had already been drawn by Dr. Livermore to the lack of bleeding from the dagger wound, *'which leads me to conclude'*, he wrote, *'that this wound was inflicted post-mortem'*. Constable frowned in disbelief. How could that be? There would have been no opportunity to stab Sir Richard after the gunshot was heard, even if whoever fired the gun was minded to do so. The time lag was so short before somebody arrived on the scene, and in any event, what would be the point in doing so? He read on.

The doctor's notes on the shotgun wound again went into meticulous detail, but the result was very much a confirmation of what he had given as a verbal estimate during the detectives' visit to his lab. The gun had been fired from approximately ten feet from where Sir Richard had been seated. Constable attempted to visualise the murder scene. Logically, with the victim in position behind his desk and facing the window, the only place the shooter could have stood was in the opening of the french windows. That certainly made sense – following the shooting, the gun could obviously have swiftly been disposed of in the lily pond in which it had been found. And with any luck at all, SOCO might manage to lift some fingerprints from it which could identify who last handled the weapon. But Constable was puzzled by the doctor's failure to state categorically that the shot had been the cause of Sir Richard's death. There was instead a repeat of the evasive reply he had given to the inspector previously. But if the shot didn't kill him, the inspector asked himself, what did? And then, why shoot him at all?

The blow to the dead man's head was the next to be analysed, in tandem with a wealth of technical data and comparative measurements which led to the conclusion that Sir Richard's own walking stick had indeed been used to assault him. Again, the doctor's report was larded with caveats, but did admit that such a wound could easily have been capable of causing death, although the precise time-frame was left open to interpretation. No great surprise there, thought Constable. But what did need explanation was the disappearance of the stick from the study and its spontaneous replacement in the hall subsequently. When, and by whom?

The comments on the apparent strangulation of the victim were equally opaque, filled with references to small bones in the throat and the presence or absence of pinpoints of blood in various locations around Sir Richard's face. I hope the court can make more sense of these than I can when we get this to trial, thought the inspector. Abstruse medical details have never been my *forte*. But at least the mechanical details were clear enough – careful measurement of the dimensions of the dog lead and a close comparison of these with the marks around Sir Richard's neck proved beyond doubt that this was the item used in the attack. This answered at least one question in the inspector's mind – it had seemed implausible that a man like Sir Richard would have casually thrown down the lead to lie where it fell. Which of course left the one crucial question. Who had handled it last? But the final words of the report on this topic were the ones that threw Constable's mind into turmoil. The doctor concluded that, while an attempt to throttle Sir Richard had certainly been made, it had failed. Strangulation had not been the cause of death. So where on earth did it fit into the pattern of other events?

A tap came at the door. "Sir? The phone logs you wanted."

The inspector looked up from his musings. An enthusiastic-looking young uniformed officer stood in the doorway.

"That was quick. Your guy said about an hour."

The P.C. glanced at his watch. "Just under, sir. We don't like to keep the people at the sharp end waiting." He held out a folder. "I'm afraid there are quite a lot, sir."

"I'd better make a start then, hadn't I? Thank you, P.C. ...?"

"Patel, sir."

"And please pass on my thanks to your team for the quick work."

"I will, sir."

Constable opened the folder in front of him and blinked slightly at the contents. They were copious. With a faint sigh, he set to work perusing them. After a few moments, he reached for Dave Copper's notebook, opened it alongside the first spread of documents, and began to work though what looked as if it was going to be a long and tedious task of comparison.

Some considerable while later, the inspector was absently reaching for the sandwich alongside the cup of tea which he had asked to be sent up from the canteen when the phone on his desk rang.

"Is that Inspector Constable?"

"It is."

"Can you hold on a moment, please." Sniff. "I have Miss Robson-Bilkes for you." Several clicks, followed by Susan's voice. "Mr. Constable? Good afternoon."

"Good grief. Is it?"

"It's certainly afternoon, inspector. Whether it's good or not is a matter I leave up to you." There was even the tiniest hint of unexpected amusement in the solicitor's voice.

"What can I do for you, Miss Robson-Bilkes?"

"It's more a matter of what I can do for you, inspector. When you came to my office, you exhibited a great deal of interest in the contents of Sir Richard Effingham's will. So as a courtesy, I am calling to let you know the arrangements for the reading of the will following the funeral."

"Which takes place tomorrow, I believe."

"That is correct. The service has been arranged for ten o'clock tomorrow morning at Knaggs End church. I gather that proceedings will be brief, so the reading of the document will take place at ten-thirty."

"At Effingham Hall, I presume?"

"No, inspector. That would of course be one

of the customary options, but when I discussed the matter with Lady Olivia Effingham, she enquired as to who would be present. I explained that it was usual for the legatees to be invited to attend, but when I informed her who these might be, she expressed an unwillingness to have certain ... parties under her roof."

"Ah." Constable allowed himself a small quiet smile. "I'm guessing that Mrs. Sarah Wadsworth might not have been a particularly welcome guest at the Hall."

"I'm afraid I could not possibly comment on that, inspector."

"So what exactly will be happening?"

"I have offered the services of the conference room here at chambers. It is quite large enough, and as we are only a short walk from the church, it seemed the most convenient solution. And it occurred to me that knowledge of the precise contents of the will might be of use to you in your investigation, and that you might like to be present. In a purely informal capacity as an observer, of course."

There was a note of surprise evident in the inspector's voice. "That really is extremely kind of you, Miss Robson-Bilkes. I have to say that, after our last meeting, I got the impression that you were rather reluctant to give us any more information than was absolutely necessary."

"Please don't misunderstand me, inspector," replied Susan. "My first duty is almost always the protection of my client's interests." A softening of tone. "But don't imagine, because we sit on opposite

215

sides of the desk, that your priorities and mine are necessarily in conflict."

"Devotion to justice trumps all, eh? Is that it?"

"Something of the sort, inspector. So, shall I expect you tomorrow?"

"I shall be there. And thank you once again."

As he replaced the receiver, Constable turned his attention once more to the papers spread before him, the sheets of phone records becoming steadily more covered by deletions in marker pen as he worked his way through the listings and succeeded in ruling out those items which were plainly irrelevant. Comparisons were made. Timings were checked. Again and again the inspector referred to the jottings in Copper's notebook, leafing backwards and forwards as he sought to dovetail the various pieces of testimony from the people the detectives had interviewed. Every so often he broke off to gaze unfocussed into the middle distance, evidently turning over matters in his mind. Finally, he sat back with a deep sigh, and a slow quiet smile spread across his face. After a moment he took a sip of his by now stone cold tea, grimaced, and then leant forward, placed a plain sheet of paper in front of himself, reached for a pen, and began to make notes.

The sudden ringing of his phone broke his concentration.

"Constable."

"Hello, guv," came the jubilant tones of his junior colleague. "Result!"

"From which I take it," smiled Constable, "that the day has gone well."

"Couldn't have been better, sir. All done and

dusted – five years, which wiped the smile off our villain's face a treat, and the judge had some very nice things to say about the way the case was handled."

"Well done you."

"So now we're just out of court. I wondered if you wanted me back there."

"Actually, sergeant, I've been managing very well in your absence. In fact, I think we're almost there. Just one or two little pieces to put into the jigsaw, and I'm sure we can wrap it up."

"That's great, sir. Er ... did you hear back from SOCO?"

"Not as yet. That's one of my jigsaw pieces, although I think I know where it's going to fit in. But of course, if you'd like to get in touch with your friend Sergeant Singleton to hurry things along ..."

"No, I'm fine, guv," came the slightly embarrassed reply. "So what's the plan?"

"We're off to a funeral tomorrow morning. Pick out a sober tie, and I'll see you here at the usual time."

"Righty-ho, guv." Copper disconnected.

Within seconds, the phone rang again. Constable picked the receiver up with a smile. "Forget something, sergeant?"

"Sorry, sir?" The voice was that of Una Singleton.

It took Constable a second or two to identify the caller. "Ah, Singleton. Sorry, wrong sergeant. I've just had Copper on the phone. I thought he was calling back about something."

"Sorry to disappoint you, sir."

"Not at all. In fact, I have every confidence that you aren't going to disappoint me in the slightest. I take it you're calling about the shotgun we left with you yesterday."

"That's right, sir. That, and the DNA from the hip flask. There's an email on its way to you with the full detailed analysis of that. And as for the gun, we've got a result, even though prolonged immersion in a muddy pond isn't the best way to preserve fingerprints. But there was just one set apart from the gardener. We've managed to lift some and match them up."

"Only the one other person?"

"Yes, sir."

"And that person would be ...?"

"Owen Elliott."

*

The bell of the parish church of Saint Eligius was tolling mournfully as Constable's car drew in a short distance behind the hearse in the High Street of Knaggs End.

"Just in time, guv," remarked Dave Copper. "I thought we were going to be late for the funeral. My mum always used to tell me that I'd be late for my own."

"Sir Richard probably didn't get tangled up with a flock of sheep on the way," replied Andy Constable, as the detectives watched the coffin being borne slowly through the lych gate and up the path towards the church door, followed by the black-clad figure of Lady Olivia Effingham, with James Booker-Gresham in slightly nervous attendance. "Actually, I'm quite glad we didn't get here too early," he

218

added, as the cortège disappeared into the building. "I didn't want to attract too much attention in advance. This way, everybody else is already in there, and we can tuck into the back of the church unobtrusively. I suspect there's going to be more than enough excitement later."

The service was short and businesslike. Two hymns were sung hesitantly by the thinly-scattered congregation, which consisted chiefly of individuals Constable recognised, together with a few unfamiliar faces who, he presumed, were locals. James mumbled a bible reading. The vicar gave a eulogy which was so general in its tone that, Constable suspected, it was drawn from a standard prepared text with the appropriate names inserted. At last, the proceedings drew to a close, and the mourners filed out of the church to stand around uncertainly in the churchyard, leaving the coffin alone on its catafalque for later interment in the Effingham family vault beneath the nave.

As the detectives emerged into the daylight, they came face-to-face with a figure formally dressed in a black business suit, topped off with a slightly incongruous black straw picture hat.

"Miss Robson-Bilkes," Constable greeted her. "I thought I saw you in the church, although I couldn't be certain, on account of the ..." He tailed off, and gestured wordlessly to the solicitor's headwear.

"Oh, this," replied Susan dismissively. "I hate hats, but one is expected to preserve some of the niceties at a funeral."

"I was hoping to run into you, so that I could

check exactly what is happening now."

"I'm just about to have a word with Lady Olivia," replied the solicitor, "to suggest that she and the other interested parties might like to make their way over to my chambers as soon as is convenient, so that I can proceed with the reading of Sir Richard's will."

"Excellent. And if it is all right by you, Sergeant Copper and I will stay well in the background, and then tag along at the end. And I hope you won't be professionally offended if I should find it necessary to interrupt your proceedings at some point."

Susan gave the inspector a long and calculating look. "Are you saying what I think you're saying, Mr. Constable?" A level gaze was the only reply. "Very well. It seems I am in your hands. But with decorum, if you please."

"So come on, guv, spill the beans," said Copper in an undertone, as Susan moved away to speak to the group surrounding Lady Olivia. "You wouldn't talk about it in the car, but I reckon you've got it all sussed, haven't you?"

"Without wishing to rush our fences, I do believe I have, sergeant."

"Was it that last bit of information from Una ... er ... Sergeant Singleton that clinched it, sir?"

"What the young lady told me was certainly very helpful," replied Constable. "I dare say you'll find an opportunity to thank her on my behalf."

"So, what's the verdict then, guv?" persisted Copper, ducking the inspector's amused speculations. "What was it all about? One of Sir

Richard's unstable relationships? Or was there some kind of turf war going on?"

Constable refused to be drawn. "You probably won't believe it yourself. To be perfectly frank, I'm not absolutely sure that I do. But it is the only way that everything fits together. And as somebody very clever once pointed out, once you have eliminated the impossible, then whatever remains, however improbable, must be the truth. Come along. Let's go and test the theory."

The group in the churchyard was beginning to gravitate towards the lych gate, and the detectives followed in their wake.

Chapter 15

The atmosphere in the conference room at the chambers of Cheetham and Partners was tense. At the head of the long highly-polished table, evidently the dining table from the time when the house had been a wealthy gentleman's residence, sat Susan Robson-Bilkes, a shiny-faced clerk who looked scarcely old enough to be out of school at her side, a portentous metal box bearing the legend 'Effingham' in elaborate cursive script lying before her. Ranged around the table was a ring of faces Constable knew well – the stern and upright figure of Lady Olivia Effingham, jaw set and eyes fixed ahead, seemingly determined not to recognise the presence of Sarah Wadsworth at the opposite end. Alongside Lady Olivia, James Booker-Gresham sat, fidgeting with his fingers. Further down the same side of the table, Pelham cast frequent watchful glances at Elspeth Carruthers, who held a handkerchief in one hand with which she occasionally wiped an eye, while beside her, looking most uncomfortable in an unaccustomed suit with collar and tie, sat Elias Diggory. Opposite James was the plump and perspiring figure of Simon Worcester, his eyes darting from one member of the company to another, and next to him, Julia Baverstock wore a stylish designer dress which looked more suited to a theatre matinée than a funeral. And after a slight gap, the languid figure of Sarah Wadsworth in a striking purple outfit, and in the chair next to hers, the slight frame of Owen Elliott, tension evident in every muscle. Andy

Constable and Dave Copper, having followed the others into the room, took a pair of seats along the wall by the door, scarcely noticed by the rest. An edgy silence reigned.

Susan poured a glass of water from the cut-glass jug in front of her, cleared her throat, and began. "Thank you all for coming, ladies and gentlemen. As you know, I have invited you all here as being the persons who have some interest in the dispositions regarding the estate of the late Sir Richard Effingham. Does anyone have any questions at this stage?" Other than a fierce flash of eyes from Lady Olivia in the direction of the foot of the table, there was no reaction. "Very well. Then we will proceed to the reading of the will." With a slightly theatrical gesture, she opened the box before her, drew out a substantial official-looking document, unfolded it, put on a pair of heavy-rimmed glasses, and prepared to read.

"Forgive me, Miss Robson-Bilkes." Constable stood and made his way to the head of the table alongside Susan. "I think it may be better to interrupt you now, before you have a chance to go into the provisions of Sir Richard's will." Nine pairs of eyes were focussed on the inspector with varying degrees of puzzlement. "And the reason I do so is that, as executor, I believe you will be tasked with obtaining probate, and what I have to say may well complicate that process. Because, as I am sure you know, there is a provision in law which states that a criminal shall not be permitted to benefit from the crime for which they were responsible. And I think that this fact is going to make more than one person

223

at this table feel uneasy."

Lady Olivia spoke up. "Are you telling us, Mr. Constable, that whoever killed my husband is here, in this room?"

"I'm afraid that is exactly what I am saying, your ladyship."

"But ... you say more than one person. I ... I'm not sure I understand you."

Constable gave a small dry smile. "I can't say I blame you, Lady Olivia. Because what we have here is an extremely complex series of events. And in reaching my conclusions, I have had to make some deductions for which I have no direct evidence, but I believe that there can be no other way in which the occurrences of the day on which Sir Richard died can have come about." He drew a small notepad from his pocket and consulted it briefly.

"Of course, the story begins well before that day. Some of the threads of it go back fifteen years ... twenty ... perhaps in some cases more. But I think it is probably most appropriate to begin with the event that precipitated the final chain of events. I'm speaking of the recent death of Mrs. Baverstock's horse 'Last Edition' in an accident at the training stables. That was the most obvious cause of the conflict between Sir Richard and, obviously, Mrs. Baverstock who believed that her interests had been inadequately taken care of, but also Mr. Elliott, who was blamed for the accident. But there was a third person who came to feel the backwash of the accident. Mr. Worcester was the man responsible for the administration of the stables' affairs, and Mrs. Baverstock's allegations also placed him in a very awkward position with Sir Richard.

"So then we turn to the events of the day in question. There were various comings and goings to Effingham Hall early on that day. Mr. Booker-Gresham and Mrs. Baverstock were involved in these, and we have a fairly clear idea of what was occurring there." James tensed and cast a frightened glance at Constable, but relaxed slightly as it became apparent that the inspector did not intend to go into any more detail at that stage. "So we will leave those aside for now. I am more interested in the sequence of visits from the afternoon onwards. Let's start at around 4.30pm. We know that Sir Richard had a meeting with Mr. Worcester in the library. Mr. Worcester claims that it was simply to dispose of some routine paperwork, but this doesn't exactly tally with the words overheard by others at the time. I believe that meeting had a very different purpose. I think Sir Richard confronted his business partner with Mrs. Baverstock's allegations over the dead horse's insurance, or rather, lack of it. I am guessing that Mr. Worcester admitted his financial mismanagement – after all, he confessed as much to us when we interviewed him. He also told us that he asked for time to put matters right. He gave us the impression that Sir Richard was mollified by this. But what if he weren't? What if, instead, he felt betrayed by the actions of an old school friend he had trusted, and was adamant that he would not tolerate the situation. Perhaps he might well have gone as far as threatening to contact the police with charges of fraud against Mr. Worcester. It would be entirely understandable. And that, some might think, would provide a plausible motive for Mr. Worcester to murder his partner."

Simon's face seemed even shinier than normal. "All right, inspector." He mopped his forehead. "It's true, Richard was absolutely furious about what had happened. He was beyond reasonable. And yes, he did utter some threats, but I thought that once he'd cooled down, he'd think better of them. That's why I called him up later. I told you. But all too late, of course."

"As you've said, sir." Constable gave a small dry cough. "Miss Robson-Bilkes, I wonder if I might trouble you for a glass of water. Talking is rather thirsty work." Wordlessly, Susan complied with the request and, after taking a sip, the inspector cast a ranging look around the table. "So now we move on to the events of the evening, and this is where things begin to gather pace.

"I've been taking a look at the telephone logs of all the people involved in this case. They provide some very instructive reading. For example, we already knew that Owen Elliott had phoned Sir Richard early in the evening. The logs confirm this – the call was timed at two minutes to seven. We have been told what was said during that call, but I suggest that the version which Mr. Elliott gave us was substantially edited. It may be a leap of faith on my part, but I now believe there was a great deal more to the conversation than Mr. Elliott has admitted, or else why would he then set out to visit Sir Richard later? I think that, during that call, Owen revealed that he knew what Sir Richard believed had up to then been a secret between himself and

Owen's mother – that Owen was Sir Richard's illegitimate son."

An outraged "What?" burst from the lips of Lady Olivia. After a venomous look in Owen's direction, she clamped her lips firmly together and stared straight ahead, while all the others, after a brief shocked glance towards the individuals at opposite ends of the room, suddenly found something of great interest in the tabletop before them. Owen flushed, but did not otherwise react.

Undeterred by the interruption, Constable continued. "Yes, Owen begged to be reinstated at that time, as he told us. Sir Richard was adamant. But it seems that he had his will to hand – quite why, we shall come on to. And in that will ..." He gestured to the document lying in front of Susan Robson-Bilkes. "... and most probably in this will, since I know of no alterations, Owen is to receive a legacy of one hundred thousand pounds from the estate." A murmured gasp of surprise, instantly stilled, rose from the company. "Sir Richard, in all probability, told him of this, but again, what if there was a threat? What if Sir Richard threatened, in the light of events, that he would seriously consider changing his will if Owen persisted? Might that not have given Owen two reasons to go to Effingham Hall that evening? One, to attempt to persuade his father to relent? Or two, to forestall his intention of removing a financial lifeline by bringing Sir Richard's own life to an end?"

"But I ... I ..."

Constable lifted a hand to halt Owen's stammerings. "Whatever may have been the

227

contents of that telephone call, it was by no means the end of the story. Because just a few minutes later ...” He took another look at his notes. “... at two minutes past seven, came the call from Sarah Wadsworth. And why did she call? I think it was to tell Sir Richard that she had got wind that he was involved with a new ... lady friend.” A snort of derision from Lady Olivia. “And I think Sir Richard admitted the fact, and told her that he was ending the relationship between himself and Mrs. Wadsworth. Perhaps he tried to pacify her. Maybe by mentioning the provisions of his will. Perhaps he even asked her to visit him with the intention of smoothing matters over. Or perhaps she was so enraged that she wanted a final face-to-face confrontation so that she could have the final word. Whichever of these is true, it certainly led to Mrs. Wadsworth's later visit. But what neither she nor Sir Richard knew was that their conversation was overheard.”

“I knew that damned man was an eavesdropper!” burst out Sarah, with an accusing glare towards Pelham. “Listening in on the call, probably. People should mind their own business instead of snooping into other people's affairs!”

“Please don't charge Mr. Pelham unjustly, Mrs. Wadsworth,” broke in Constable. “This was nothing to do with him. On the contrary, the person who overheard Sir Richard's end of the conversation was, in fact, Lady Olivia.”

The reaction was a frosty look from the lady. “Are you accusing me of deliberately spying on my husband, Mr. Constable?”

"Oh, perhaps not deliberately, your ladyship," responded the inspector. "I'm afraid your love of gardening may have been responsible. Mr. Diggory thought he saw you pulling up some weeds in one of your favourite flowerbeds outside the library window. In all probability, that is what you set out to do. But by a stroke of coincidence, you happened to be doing it at the precise moment of the conversation between Sir Richard and Mrs. Wadsworth. And, the window being open, I suspect you heard the entire conversation. The situation between your husband and his mistress was laid bare."

Lady Olivia drew herself up. "Is there any point in your apparent intention to embarrass me publicly, Mr. Constable? I fail to see what bearing the relationships my husband may have had with other ... persons, which I have already discussed with you during an extremely humiliating conversation, can have to do with my actions on the day of his death."

"Oh, a considerable bearing, I think," rejoined Constable. "Because the point, I believe, is that this conversation was impossible to ignore. You may have been able to turn a blind eye before, but this was direct and damning evidence. The final straw in a lifetime of disloyalty by your husband. And so you decided to murder him. Who could blame you? A wife repeatedly betrayed by the man she had married. And here I take a complete leap in the dark, but no doubt you'll tell me if my suggestion of what happened next is wide of the mark. You of course knew of the existence of the rat poison in Punter's food store. You went there and decanted a quantity

229

into a small bottle. This was what you took to the drawing room, concealed in a handkerchief, when you went there for drinks before dinner. When Mrs. Carruthers left the room, you had barely enough time to add the poison to the fresh jug of water which the housekeeper had just brought, knowing that only your husband took water with his whisky, and you then poured yourself a gin and tonic before Mr. Booker-Gresham entered the room at about ten minutes to eight." Constable regarded Lady Olivia expectantly and raised his eyebrows in interrogation.

The previous hostility had vanished from Lady Olivia's voice. "I think, Mr. Constable, that if you expect me to reply, you are going to be disappointed. I think I had best say nothing before I take some advice." She cast a look towards Susan Robson-Bilkes alongside her, who despite the astounded look in her eyes, was managing to preserve an outward air of professional calm.

"I think you are wise to do so, your ladyship," said Constable. "Because the story is far from over. And who knows, perhaps if Mr. Booker-Gresham had come into the room a few moments earlier, that chapter might not even have been written. We shall never know. But arrive he did, and poured a whisky with ice for himself. And when Sir Richard arrived a few minutes later, he poured himself a whisky and water, but had not begun to drink it before Mr. Pelham came in at five past eight to tell him that he had a visitor. This was Mrs. Wadsworth, a fact of which Lady Olivia was aware, even though there was an attempt at discretion on the part of the

230

butler. So she was left in a state of nervous anticipation, wondering whether and how the poisoned drink would take effect.

"Let's leave Lady Olivia in her state of uncertainty, and follow Sir Richard to the library, where Mrs. Wadsworth was waiting. We've heard from the lady what happened during that confrontation, and I have no reason to doubt what she told me. Except for one small fact which she forgot to mention. I think the scene was brief but turbulent. Most of what had to be said, Mrs. Wadsworth's own decision to bring the relationship to an end, had already been said over the phone. We know, because she told us, that Sir Richard showed her his will which included a legacy to her of one hundred thousand pounds ..."

Eyes widened in surprise around the table. Lady Olivia, after a sudden intake of breath, remained stock-still, staring ahead impassively with a face of granite.

"If Sir Richard had hoped to pacify Mrs. Wadsworth by this action, he had gravely misjudged his audience. She snatched the will from him, set fire to it with the gold lighter which her former lover himself had given her, and flung the burning document into the unlit fireplace, discarding the lighter in the log box at the same time, and stormed out. Oh, but there was one other thing she did, which was the one piece of information she omitted to give us. Again, a guess on my part, but the only plausible explanation of what was subsequently found. She turned on the gas tap to the library log fire. Didn't you, Mrs. Wadsworth?"

"Yes, but I ..."

Constable overrode her. "Who can say what the motive for that action was? Was the fire supposed to catch in order to make sure that the will was completely consumed? It failed. The will remained only half-burnt. Was there some sort of misguided impulse for revenge, in that the gas was supposed to poison the faithless lover, or even to lead to some sort of explosion, in order to destroy Sir Richard and all his works?" Constable gave a small dry chuckle. "Yes, I grant you, the stuff of high melodrama, but even the most unlikely scenario has to be considered.

"And so, Mrs. Wadsworth left the house. Sir Richard was at that time still alive." Constable checked his notes once more. "We then come to around ten past eight and the next arrival at Effingham Hall, Mrs. Julia Baverstock, invited for dinner at what was likely to be, at best, a somewhat strained evening. But for the moment, the social niceties were preserved. Mr. Booker-Gresham offered her a drink, and poured her a sherry. He then contrived to spill some of the sherry on himself as an excuse to leave the room, just shortly after ten past eight, because he hoped then to have an excuse to replace the pilfered dagger."

"Master James?" said Elspeth Carruthers. "You took it? Oh, I'd never have believed it of you. You were always such a good boy." Pelham, alongside her, raised a doubting eyebrow.

"James!" Lady Olivia sounded outraged. "That was you? You stole from your uncle, after all we have done for you?" A horrified expression came over her face. "But if you had the dagger, what else did you do?"

James put his face into his hands. "Please, Aunt Olivia, don't," he pleaded. "I know I was a fool, but I was desperate, and I couldn't see ... I didn't know how ..." He tailed off into incoherence.

Constable took up the narration again. "Mr. Booker-Gresham has freely confessed what happened next, ladies. He says he retrieved the dagger from its hiding place in the hall, where he had temporarily concealed it on his return to the house after lunch, and went to the library. I dare say he listened at the door, but since Mrs. Wadsworth had now left, all was now quiet. Unfortunately for James, Sir Richard was still there, and James was caught red-handed. I have no doubt that a violent argument ensued, during which Sir Richard threatened to cut off all financial support and change his will, cancelling James' proposed legacy. Given the young man's precarious fiscal position, it was little short of a financial death sentence. And, as he says, he was desperate. So he acted."

"And he had the dagger."

"No, Lady Olivia," contradicted Constable. "He'd returned that to Sir Richard. I suspect your husband was keeping a very firm grip on his restored property at that moment. But I think there was, also on the desk, the dog lead. The lead which Sir Richard had put there when entering the library on his return from his afternoon walk, and which had not yet been put back in its customary place. In a moment of unreasoned behaviour, I believe that Mr. Booker-Gresham snatched up that dog lead and put it around Sir Richard's neck in an attempt to strangle him."

Subdued murmurs of astonishment arose around the table. Shocked looks were exchanged.

"However," continued the inspector, "it was an attempt only. Not a successful one. Our medical colleagues have confirmed for us that strangulation was not the cause of Sir Richard's death. In this, as apparently in so many other things, Mr. Booker-Gresham was not very competent. True, Sir Richard would have lost consciousness, which no doubt led Mr. Booker-Gresham to believe that he had been successful. And then, perhaps horrified by his own actions, he flung down the lead and fled. A car was heard. Was that James fleeing from the scene of his crime? No. He made his way upstairs, from where he later reappeared. What he did not realise was that Sir Richard had only blacked out for a few moments, and that he regained his senses shortly afterwards."

"Mr. Constable," broke in Susan Robson-Bilkes. "I have to say that I am puzzled as to where this is all leading. You seem to have brought to the house all those who were there ahead of the shooting of Sir Richard, and yet you seem to be busily exonerating people who might have been involved. With one exception, of course. And if James didn't use the knife, who did?"

"You're right, of course, Miss Robson-Bilkes," agreed Constable. "And that is precisely where I turn my attention next. Mrs. Julia Baverstock."

Chapter 16

All eyes immediately focussed on Julia.

"But Julia was with my aunt when I left the drawing room," protested James. "And she was in there when my uncle was found."

"So she was," agreed Constable. "But your aunt did not stay in the drawing room for long. She admitted as much to me. Yes, I can quite understand the explanation she gave to me, that she found it impossible to keep up the facade of pleasant sociability, especially in view of the day's earlier revelations. But there is a further explanation. She still had in her possession the bottle containing traces of the poison. She had to dispose of this. So, no doubt in a highly agitated state at the realisation of what she had done – at any moment, her husband might be drinking from his glass of whisky – she left the drawing room to go upstairs. This was at twenty past eight, according to the housekeeper, who observed Lady Olivia to be still holding the handkerchief which concealed the poison bottle. No doubt she rinsed the bottle thoroughly in her room. I suspect that in all probability we shall never find it, nor any incriminating traces in it. But her ladyship's departure left Mrs. Baverstock alone in the drawing room.

"I believe Mrs. Baverstock took advantage of that situation. She had probably been told that Sir Richard was in the library when she arrived, although I doubt very much whether Lady Olivia would have mentioned the identity of his visitor. James was presumed to be elsewhere. And so, moments after Lady Olivia left the room, Mrs. Baverstock made her way to the library where Sir Richard sat, alone as expected, in the dimly-lit room. I dare say she resumed her tirade against him. But there was no reaction. Mrs. Baverstock, you yourself told us that Sir Richard simply sat there, not responding in any way. Of course, that might be entirely plausible if he were semi-conscious. But you believed him to be ignoring you, sitting with his back to you in a contemptuous fashion. I think this was the final straw – overwhelmed with rage, you snatched up the dagger from the desk where it lay, went around to where Sir Richard was sitting with apparently uncaring eyes, and at the peak of your fury, plunged the dagger into his chest."

Gasps of horror and incredulity arose from the people seated at the table. "Julia, no!" "Oh, that's horrible!" "Madam, how could you?"

Constable held up a hand to stem the outburst. "Ladies and gentlemen, please. Startling though that may have sounded – and I apologise for the perhaps over-dramatic nature of the narration – it is not the end of the story. There are other factors we have to consider. But for the moment, Mrs. Baverstock was undoubtedly certain in her own mind that she had murdered Sir Richard. That must have been a ghastly realisation. I doubt whether she had any such thought in her mind when she arrived at the house. So, horrified and stunned by what she had done, she returned to the drawing room." The inspector allowed himself a small grim smile. "It would hardly be a surprise if, under those circumstances, she felt she needed a stiff drink."

Susan Robson-Bilkes spoke up once again. "Inspector, it seems to me that the more you tell us, the less I understand. I don't follow your repeated insistence on timings. We all know when the gun was fired. You account for all the people in the house, but you don't account for the shot which we have all assumed was what killed Sir Richard. So unless you intend to lay the blame on one of the members of staff ..."

"Nothing was further from my mind," the inspector reassured the servants, who had reacted in startled bewilderment to the solicitor's comment. "But the timings are crucial, believe me. And you say I appear to have accounted for all those in the house prior to Sir Richard's death. Not so. Appearances can be deceptive. Assumptions can be mistaken. Consider the following possible scenario.

"Owen Elliott had spoken to Sir Richard earlier. He mentioned to us his intention to plead face-to-face with his father to take pity on him, and told us that this intention was what brought him to the front door of Effingham Hall at the moment when Sir Richard's body was discovered. But consider the other possibility that, during the earlier telephone conversation, Owen's father had discounted all hope of reconsidering his decision. I offered you two possible reasons for Elliott to come to the house. What if it were the second? Might he not have come with the intention to kill Sir Richard? Or, perhaps, merely to threaten him? He knows the layout of the house and its outbuildings well. He knows where Mr. Diggory keeps his shotgun. So let me offer you the following picture. Owen comes to the house, along the path from the village through the grounds, and reaches the deserted stable yard at twenty-five past eight. He abstracts the gun, loads it, and makes his way around the house to the library windows on the north terrace, possibly seeking a way to enter the house unobserved. And it seems that chance favours his plans. The library french windows are slightly ajar. The curtains are pulled together, but not completely, and through the gap, Sir Richard is visible, seated in his swivel chair with his back to the desk, and apparently looking straight at the window where Owen's face appears. In a panic, all thoughts of threats, pleading, confrontation are forgotten. Owen fires the gun straight at Sir Richard, and immediately flees along the terrace round the west side of the house, unobserved from within because everyone's attention was focussed towards the library, and arrives at the front door as Sir Richard's body is discovered at twenty-eight minutes past eight. Again, we can time this precisely, because just one minute later, having emerged from the murder scene, Mr. Pelham is calling the police to report the incident, as verified by the telephone logs. Owen has paused in his flight to do just one thing - to fling into the lily pond the shotgun which he had used to carry out his attack. The shotgun which, when recovered, bears his fingerprints. And his alone."

After a moment of shocked silence from all those in the room, Owen broke down. "I never meant to do it," he sobbed. "It was just panic. I wasn't thinking straight. And those eyes – there was something in them. I felt he could see down into my soul. How could I have done something like that to a man who'd always treated me like a son? The son he couldn't admit to ..." He tailed off into incoherence.

Dave Copper rose silently from his chair and came to stand behind Owen. He seemed about to place a hand on the young man's shoulder but, at a signal from his superior officer, stepped back with a puzzled look.

"I think it will be quite safe to leave Mr. Elliott for a few moments, sergeant," said Constable. "It will give him a chance to recover his composure. And it will also give me a chance to complete the picture. There are details – highly significant details – which I have not yet explained. And that brings me back to the telephone logs which I mentioned a moment ago." He consulted his notes briefly once more.

"Everyone agrees that, immediately after Mr. Pelham's call to the police, a call was received at Effingham Hall from Mr. Worcester at eight thirty. This is verified from two sources – the house log which records the incoming call, and Mr. Worcester's phone log, which lists his outgoing call. Not, however, from the land-line from the stables. This call came from his mobile. And the thing about mobile telephone logs is that they do not simply record the fact and the time of the call – they very helpfully give us the information as to the phone masts through which the call was routed. And by means of some very complex trigonometrical calculations which I do not pretend to follow, our technical people have been able to place the location of the call, again not at the training stables, but at the lay-by on the main road a few yards from the

239

south lodge of Effingham Hall."

There were frowns of incomprehension around the table.

"So, now we know that Mr. Worcester's car was in the vicinity of Effingham Hall far earlier than was previously stated. That's an odd inconsistency. Here's another one. Mr. Diggory has told us that he heard a car go past his north lodge at almost exactly eight fifteen. And Mrs. Carruthers, busy in the kitchen, also heard a car some five minutes later. It doesn't take five minutes to drive from the north lodge to the stable yard at the rear of the house. So was the first sound that of the car arriving, and the second one that of it leaving? We know Mr. Booker-Gresham's car wasn't moved. Mrs. Baverstock had already arrived at the front of the house. Mrs. Wadsworth had walked up from the village. Mr. Elliott likewise. That leaves only one vehicle unaccounted for – Mr. Worcester's. Once again, the phone logs betrayed him. Because even when a phone is not in use for a call, its whereabouts can be detected, and at eight-fifteen, Mr. Worcester's phone's location is shown to have been at Effingham Hall. And not the road outside, but at the Hall itself. And you may not have noticed, in this long series of events, that one of the injuries which Sir Richard suffered has also not been mentioned. There was also additional evidence found at the scene, which has not yet been brought into the calculation. I believe that all these missing pieces of the jigsaw fit together as follows.

"At eight-fifteen, Mr. Worcester drove in, past the north lodge, and parked in the stable yard on the east side of the house. He probably coasted to a halt so as not to attract attention. He came round the house via the north terrace and peered through the gap in the curtains, leaving his footprints in the flowerbed as he did so. He saw the back of Sir Richard sitting in his desk chair, entered through the french windows, as he hoped unheard, and picked up Sir Richard's walking stick from the stand there. Sir Richard, recovering his senses from James' botched attack, turned his chair at that moment, and Mr. Worcester delivered a single massive blow to Sir Richard's temple. He left the way he came, taking with him the walking stick with its traces of Sir Richard's blood, pulling the curtains and french widows together behind him. Perhaps he paused for a moment to take a swig of whisky from his hip flask - there's DNA on the flask, and I'm prepared to wager it will show a match - but in the panic of the moment, he fumbled the flask and let it fall, to be discovered in the flower bed the following day. The hip flask bearing the engraved legend 'O.E' - not standing for Owen Elliott or Olivia Effingham, but for 'Old Edmundians' - the old boys' association of the school which he and Sir Richard had both attended. There was no time to search for the flask in the gloom of the evening. He made for his car and drove away hurriedly at eight-twenty, driving though the back lanes and parking in the lay-by near the south lodge just before eight-thirty. He phoned the Hall - his intention was probably to ask to speak to Sir Richard, so that he could ascertain the situation. But the body had just been discovered. Mr. Worcester was told that the police were on their way, which suited him very well. All he had to do was wait for the police car to arrive and tuck in behind it, so as to arrive at the house at the same time as our colleagues, demonstrably innocent of any involvement in what had occurred." Constable paused, and took another sip of water.

"So, inspector," said Susan Robson-Bilkes, "if I understand you correctly, you are saying that virtually all the people around this table, with obvious exceptions ..." A nod towards the Effingham Hall employees. "... have been responsible for attempts on Sir Richard's life. Are you serious?"

Constable took a long cool look around the table. Most of those present declined to meet his gaze. "Entirely serious, Miss Robson-Bilkes."

"But you still don't explain who precisely was responsible for his death. Not all of them, surely? Or are you advancing the theory of some fantastic conspiracy?"

"Nothing of the kind, Miss Robson-Bilkes. This is not a 1930's novel. Although I have to admit, when first considering the whole range of evidence, I was thoroughly confused by the number and nature of the injuries to the victim. But I am now entirely clear in my mind as to the identity of the person who actually killed Sir Richard, for which I am indebted to an extremely comprehensive report produced by the police doctor.

"We'll take a look at the various attempts one by one. Let's consider the attempted poisoning. It transpired that, with everything going on as it did, Sir Richard never had the chance to drink his whisky and water, as is proved by the fact that no toxins were discovered in his body. It therefore follows that, whatever Lady Olivia Effingham may have intended, she was not responsible for his death. Then there is the fact that, when Mr. Pelham discovered the body, the room was full of the smell of gas. If there is any shred of humour to be found in this situation, it is this rather farcical element. Sir Richard could never have realised that his decision to take the old domestic coal-gas plant out of commission in favour of mains gas was so prescient. Because Mrs. Wadsworth seems to have overlooked the fact that, despite all the old myths about people putting their heads into gas ovens to kill themselves, modern natural gas is completely non-poisonous.

"Then there is the attempted strangulation. Again, the doctor's report testifies that this did not lead to Sir Richard's death. Mr. James Booker-Gresham's incompetence led him to botch this assumed effort to strangle his uncle, and as Sir Richard is no longer alive to testify against him, it is unlikely that any charges will be brought. On this count, that is. There may be further investigations into his other activities, but that is not a matter for discussion at this particular moment. Suffice to say that we are watching him very carefully.

"We then come to the most obvious and most likely causes of Sir Richard's death – the dagger wound, and the shotgun blast. I should perhaps have been quicker on the uptake when I first viewed the scene of the crime, when Doctor Livermore showed me these wounds. There was relatively little bleeding, and when we spoke later he again referred to the fact that he found this puzzling. But having considered the point fully, he reached the conclusion that the lack of bleeding from the dagger wound indicated that the victim was already dead when that attack occurred. The same logic applies to the effects of the shotgun blast. Since this was self-evidently the last wound to be inflicted, it is obvious that the victim was already dead when that took place. I shall be consulting people with far greater legal knowledge than my own, but it seems to me that, whatever crime Mrs. Julia Baverstock and Mr. Owen Elliott may have committed, it certainly wasn't murder.

"However, the medical report confirms that the blow to Sir Richard's head brought about a massive brain haemorrhage which resulted in almost instant death. A death which would mean that the ownership of the stables would revert to the sole surviving member of the partnership, and which would bring an end to any immediate questions regarding financial mismanagement or impropriety. There would have been precious time to find a solution to the problems and avoid the consequences. A valuable motive, both in monetary and personal terms. So, with that motive in mind – with the forensic evidence of the means whereby the crime was committed – and with the technical evidence which proves that he was present at the scene at the crucial moment, I am now placing Mr. Simon Worcester under arrest for murder. Sergeant Copper, would you please take charge of Mr. Worcester."

During the latter part of the inspector's narrative, Simon had slumped lower and lower in his seat in the face of the inevitability of the approaching conclusion. As Constable finished, Simon lifted his head and looked around the company. "I always felt he looked down on me," he said quietly, his voice devoid of emotion. "Even at school. Because of who he was and who I was – just the son of a tradesman with enough money to send his son to a good school. Oh, nothing was ever said – he was far too well-bred for that. We were actually quite good friends. Perhaps I was too sensitive. And then, years later, when we met again, he offered me the position in the business. I was perfect, he said – he came from the world of horses and I came from money, so I would understand all the things he never would. Was there even some sort of implicit sneer in that? I don't know. But it worked well over the years – until a few things went wrong. I started to gamble – well, why not use the knowledge I thought I had? But it turned out I was never as clever as I thought I was. I made losses. So I tried to cover them by gambling even bigger sums. It never works. So I started to use the money from the business, and then there was sometimes a problem with meeting commitments and paying bills, but somehow I managed to hold it all together – that is, until this business with Julia's horse brought everything to a head. And when Richard confronted me with it, it all came pouring out – his contempt for me and my obsession with money. Barrow-boy mentality, he called it. He said he could forgive everything except a betrayal of trust. Him! With his record of behaviour! So there it was. I was faced with ruin. Prison. No way out. And so, inspector, I did exactly what you have so very cleverly worked out." He looked again at those seated round the table. "Not that I expect any sympathy. But none of you here should be too quick to condemn me." His voice took on a harder note. "Because you all know very well, if what Inspector Constable tells us is true, that you are all just as guilty as me. You all hated Richard. You all wanted him dead. And if it hadn't been for me, one of you would be in my place. So you'd better take a minute to spare a thought for yourselves." He stood, and a bitter smile twisted his face. "Who knows? Maybe we'll all meet again in court."

At a nod from Constable, Copper placed a hand on Simon's shoulder and guided him from the room. The inspector made to follow, but paused in the doorway to look back at the ring of faces, silent and with a variety of expressions ranging from shock to incredulity.

"Miss Robson-Bilkes," he said, "it may not be up to me, but in the light of what you've heard, you may wish to suspend proceedings for today and seek some further guidance as to the legal standing of some of the provisions of Sir Richard's will. And as for the remainder of you ..." His eyes rested on each person in turn. "... we will be in touch with you all very soon. And I suggest that, before we do, some of you may wish to ask Miss Robson-Bilkes if she can recommend a good defence lawyer."

The door closed behind him with an ominous finality.

*

Dave Copper dunked the digestive biscuit in

his tea. He shook his head in wonderment. "I'm still trying to get my brain around it all, guv," he said.

"In what way, sergeant?" enquired Andy Constable. He smiled. "I would have thought that, after this morning's little session, it would all be crystal clear to you."

Copper gave his superior a wry look. "Maybe if I had a Ph.D. in looniness, guv. You have to admit, it was all a bit mad. What, six people all deciding that they'd had enough of the victim and all making up their minds to do him in on the same day in the same place? I mean, they might have thought they all had good reason, so you could say it was odds on that the poor guy was going to get killed eventually, but it's not exactly murder by the book, is it?"

"You have a point," admitted Constable. "Maybe that just proves that I have the bizarre sort of brain that can visualise these weird scenarios. Which is bound to come in handy avoiding the pitfalls if I ever decide to take up a life of crime – on the other side of the desk, that is." He took a sip of his own tea, leaned back in his chair, and stretched his arms above his head. "Goodness. That's the first time in a long time that that didn't actually hurt."

"Great. Back to normal then, sir."

Constable chuckled. "If you can call this case normal."

"So come on then, guv. Tell all. I wish I'd been around when you figured it all out, instead of cooling my heels in court for most of the day. So what was the light-bulb moment?"

Constable considered for a few seconds. "I suppose I must have got an inkling of it when we were going around talking to everyone. There was some sort of mixture of defiance and relief in what most of them said, which must have been down to the fact that they were all convinced that they were off the hook because the gunshot was what killed Sir Richard. Certainly Owen Elliott believed that he was the killer, which is most probably why he went to pieces far more than the others. But once it was clear that it wasn't the shot that was fatal – and really we should have all picked that up on the spot from the limited amount of bleeding, except that we were all distracted by all the other wounds – then we obviously had to look elsewhere. And 'elsewhere', for which the Latin word is of course *alibi*, turned out to be another crucial concept – all the others were on the scene apart from Simon Worcester, who had a particularly helpful alibi. What do I always say to you? Never trust an unbreakable alibi. And as for motivation, everyone else had what they thought was just and reasonable cause to hate Sir Richard, but Simon Worcester was the only one under immediate threat. As he said, ruin, and probably prison." The inspector shrugged. "It just all fitted together."

"I could never have done it in a hundred years, guv," remarked Copper admiringly. "Absolute genius."

"Yes, well, enough of that," replied his superior gruffly. "I don't have the time to sit around chatting, and neither do you. Don't forget, we have some very complicated unravelling to do. I need to have a good long chat with our legal people to see what charges if any we're going to want to bring against all the Knaggs End crowd, and then you and I are no doubt going to have to generate a frightening quantity of paperwork."

"Terrific, guv. Your favourite part of the job." Copper sighed. "I suppose we'd better get on with it, then. And knowing my luck, it's going to take forever."

"We'd better not be too long about it," said Constable. "You never know what the next phone call is going to bring."

The two detectives laughed and looked at the telephone on Constable's desk. After a few moments, it began to ring.

*   *   *

THE INSPECTOR CONSTABLE MURDER MYSTERIES

MURDERER'S FETE
(First published in paperback as Fêted To Die)
Constable and Copper investigate the death of a celebrity clairvoyant at the annual garden fête at Dammett Hall

MURDER UNEARTHED
(First published in paperback as Juan Foot In The Grave)
A lucky win takes Constable and Copper on holiday to Spain, but murder soon rears its head among the British community on the Costa

DEATH SAILS IN THE SUNSET
Our detectives find themselves aboard a brand new cruise liner, but swiftly discover that some guilty secrets refuse to be buried at sea.

MURDER COMES TO CALL
A trio of cases for Constable and Copper to tackle - in 'Death By Chocolate', the victim comes to a sticky end at Wally Winker's Chocolate Factory; in 'The Dead Of Winter', there's first degree murder at Harde-Knox College; and in 'Set For Murder', there's a grisly shock in store at the Spanner House of Horror film studios.

MURDER MOST FREQUENT
Three more challenging cases for the detecting duo -
in 'Murder On The Rocks', the knives are out at the Palais de Glace restaurant; can the show go on when 'Death Waits In The Wings' at the Queen's Theatre?; and in 'Last Orders', a village pub fun run takes an unexpected course.

www.rogerkeevil.co.uk

Printed in Great Britain
by Amazon